GIFTED

The First Book of THE GUARDIANS SAGA

WRITTEN BY: MYLAN ALLEN
COVER ART BY: TYSON KINGSBURY

Story: April 8th, 2013—April 27th, 2014

ACKNOWLEDGEMENTS

First, I would like to say thank you to my wonderful family who put up with me holed up in my room, writing all the time, and taking me to the store to buy more books to inspire me to do more writing. Thank you for all of the love and support that you all have given me, it is *greatly* appreciated!

Secondly, thank you to Aaron Cooze and Maya Marcus for proofreading, plot ideas and helping me keep the story less crowded and direct to the point. I would also like to say an ENORMOUS thank you to Tyson Kingsbury for taking time out of his busy schedule to proof-read the novel and design the wonderful cover.

Lastly, I'd like to thank my favourite authors and writers for inspiration and who directed my love for the Supernatural: *Jerry Siegel, Joe Shuster, Rick Riordan, Robert Kirkman, Geoff Johns, Marion G. Harmon, Wesley King, Pittacus Lore, D.J Machale, James Patterson and The Immortal Stan Lee.*

Ten years ago, superheroes were everywhere. Some could fly, some were super strong and some had more power than anyone could even imagine. There was one team of heroes that everyone loved, respected and looked up to more than any other superhero or superhero team, The Titans. They consisted of 12 members who risked their lives for strangers on a daily basis. All until members of their own team turned on them.

Atlas and Marvella were the Earth's greatest protectors, even though they were publically known as aliens, they were accepted. Immortales, a human that was cursed with immortality lead the corrupted and mind-controlled, members into battle against Atlas, Marvella, Mercury and Artemis, the teams' only uncorrupted members. Mercury used his super speed to his advantage; dodging punches just as fast as he could throw them while Artemis fired arrows everywhere until they were eventually overcome.

That left Atlas and Marvella. They put up good fights, but Atlas lost it when his notorious partner, also the mother of his child was murdered. Three out of the four most iconic and most experienced members were inevitably beaten…

Atlas beat every single villain that went up against him in a fit of rage. He worked his best, didn't hold anything back and put every single villain in a secure government facility. As he reached a good-gone-bad old teammate, *Immortales*, he stole Atlas' abilities using magic, his only true weakness. The now powerless Arthur Zimmerman was left to raise his son, Arion, on his own.

Ten years ago, the civilians protested against the heroes. People were killed, the damage to the cities was monumental and superheroes were shamed to near-extinction. That day, the superheroes stopped being super and continued their normal lives. Most of them even lost their powers...

Ten years ago, they never could have imagined the new age of **gifted** heroes and villains that would come to take their places...

CHAPTER I: FORMATION

1. TITAN

rion groggily awoke to the sounds of his dad calling from downstairs, "YOU'LL BE LATE FOR SCHOOL, SON! IT'S FRIDAY, BE HAPPY!" Arion got ready for school and pulled on his clothes, preparing for the summer weather.

After he combed his short black hair and brushed his teeth, he nearly *flew* down the stairs. "Happy Birthday!" his dad called. He ran his chocolate brown hand through his own small afro, as if he was scared or worried, but his blue eyes were glistening with pride and happiness, "My boy turns 15!"

"Yeah, yeah. Thanks." Arion walked over to the cupboard to get some cereal.

"Are you kidding me?" his dad demanded. "You're not having cereal! I've been in the kitchen for over an hour!"

After they ate bacon, omelets and pancakes, Arion finished getting ready and left his small, country-style house in nearly the middle of nowhere, and began walking to his bus stop. The day went by quicker than he had expected and school was done before he knew it.

After all of the birthday beats, he was sure that his arm would be bruised the next day, his caramel coloured skin bruised easily.

When he got home his dad was already there. Since he was a full-time author, he stayed at home for most of the day while he was writing. He had a huge grin on his face going from ear-to-ear.

"There's something that I need to show you," he announced. He walked into the living room while Arion slung his bag off of his shoulder and onto the floor. It was just a typical family room, with a couple of chairs, couches, a computer, a desk and a TV with a bookshelf surrounding it, where they kept movies and books.

His dad punched in a sequence of numbers on a hidden keypad, beside the shelf *102299*. The bookshelf slid to the right smoothly leaving an open space. They walked into it and the bookshelf slid back into place in front of them.

They began to move, smoothly, barely detectable. The elevator lowered itself for about thirty seconds. When the bell dinged, the doors opened showing a huge bright white room. The room was lined up with 13 floor-to-ceiling glass tubes, five on the left, five on the right and three in front of them.

The five on either side were empty so Arion focused on the three glass tubes ahead of them and jogged there while his dad just strolled behind him.

The first tube had a costume in it. The costume was a mixture of cobalt and sky blue with white highlights and a picture of a glowing, yellow sun in the center, fit with a blue cape. It had matching boots designed with both blues with white lines crossing it in a pattern. On the mannequin's face was a pair of light blue sunglasses with dark lenses.

Arion looked back at his dad and he was scratching his goatee and looking around as if he hadn't been down there in a long time. Arion turned back to look at the suit and recognized it. It was the costume of the world's *first* real superhero, the one who nearly invented the career of being a superhero all those years ago, *Atlas*.

Two tubes down was another costume. The costume of *Marvella*, the world's first female superhero. Her costume was nearly identical to Atlas's except it was dark red and scarlet red with white highlights and a glowing, white moon on the front, also fit with a cape, except shorter and red.

"You're..." Arion stammered looking back at his dad.

"Yes, I'm—err—I *was,* Atlas."

"That is... wait. Does that mean," he pointed to Marvella's costume. "She was..."

"Yes, she was your mother. We may not have been married, but you are the son of Atlas and Marvella. *Happy Birthday.*"

"No *FREAKING* WAY!" Arion yelled. "So you're telling me...that I am *literally* the kid of the two most *powerful* alien superheroes on the planet!? How cool did you expect me to be with all of this!?"

"Well, umm," his dad stuttered. "I was hoping that you'd be pretty cool with it."

"This...this isn't even *possible!* I'm so normal and you guys were so...*super!*"

"Maybe you'll be super too one day," his dad muttered under his breath.

After Arion had calmed down, he asked tons of questions. He

learned that he is half-*Zonarian* (from his dad) and half-*Lyriic* (from his mom,) which made him a *double* alien hybrid, not even remotely human. His parent's sources of abilities was any type of radiation, whereas their weaknesses were *extreme* vulnerabilities to magic and not being able to absorb radiation.

"Zonarians and Lyriics were among the first races to colonize Earth," his dad told him. "That's why we have no notable differences from humans. But, let's just say the war between our races *may* have...killed the dinosaurs. But that's another story!"

He told Arion the story of how his mother actually died and how she wasn't killed in a random construction accident, like everyone else was lead to believe. Then he told him how he gave up his own abilities and how all of the heroes split up and lived their separate, non-superhero, lives.

"Will I get superpowers?" Arion demanded excitedly.

"I'm not too sure. Your mother and I were from completely separate worlds and were both exposed to the earth's atmosphere at different times. We didn't even know if we could...cross-breed with these powers." They were sitting at a professional, board-meeting style table in a room just off of the costume room. "Your mother's planet was probably destroyed, unlike mine which isn't too far from it, and probably still intact."

He had already shown Arion the ships earlier. The first was more of a frosted glass, and was almost shaped like a sports car. But, the second one was smaller, fit for a baby, maybe and was clear as a crystal. "If you develop powers, they will most likely be mine, or a mixture between the two because Zonarians have always overpowered the Lyriics and all half-breeds were destroyed upon the planetary rulers' discovery." Arion's horrified look made his dad say, "Dictators are overrated."

"Oh...well on that happy note!" Arion said, still not fully convinced.

"Yep..." his dad trailed off. "Your powers should begin to develop around your 15ᵗʰ birthday, if you take after me. And all of this is *if* you get them at all so...that's why I decided to tell you on today of all days."

His dad showed him around their *lair*. It had a personal gym, with adjustable weights capable of going up into the thousands of tons, treadmills capable of taking speeds faster than most sports cars, and robots capable of taking what nearly any super strong superhero could dish out. The rooms' walls were laced with solar-based panels, therefore with the push of a button it could emit stronger solar rays or absorb them, to leave Atlas or Marvella powerless to train them better. That would explain why his dad had muscles. The lair was expanded under the unused land and gave them a whole bunch of space.

"I have a few tests to run!" his dad said, walking away. "If you get powers, you need to be prepared and I need to make sure that you stay prepared...for anything. Feel free to look around a bit more, I'll meet you in about a half-hour in the costume room."

2.   QUANTUM

Lucian Lieber was a *brilliant* teenager but didn't show it at all when he was at school, usually just passing with 60's or 70's. He could build nearly anything if he had the money, resources and time. No one would ever think that he lived in a group home with tons of other *siblings*, being mistreated, he was just too nice and funny.

Lucian was sitting in his tiny, almost closet-sized room, eating some crackers and cheese, a simple snack. When he finished he jogged down the creaking wooden staircase, downstairs to the kitchen. He dropped the plate into the sink before leaving to go back to his room. *Owen*, the *father* of the group home family noticed him leaving.

Owen was a huge man, he probably weighed about 380 pounds and was six-foot-6. He was so wide that he had to turn *sideways* to walk through doorways. He had a small tuft of brown hair on the top of his head and the sides were shaved, just like the rest of his face.

"Lucian!" he screamed. Lucian turned around, cringing. "How many times do I have to tell you," he raised his hand and the back of it connected with Lucian's pale skin. The swelling around his blue eyes had just finished healing from the last time one of the people that were *supposed* to be protecting him, had hit him.

They called it *discipline*, or *God's will*. Lucian couldn't even believe that there *was* a God. No one—no matter *how* powerful—could be that cruel to a bunch of kids who couldn't defend themselves from monsters like this.

Lucian fell to the floor and put his hand on his stinging face. "DO THE DISHES ONCE YOU'RE FINISHED WITH THEM!" he bellowed at the fifteen-year old. Lucian was too stunned to say anything. He had hit him for forgetting to do the dishes. That's what his life had been like for the past 11 years. "DO YOU SEE ANY OTHER DISHES IN THE SINK!? HOW WILL YOU EVER BECOME A MAN IF YOU CAN'T EVEN CLEAN UP *AFTER* YOURSELF!?"

Owen grabbed Lucian's arm, and dragged him up the stairs before throwing him onto to the floor of his bedroom. Lucian sat on the wooden floor of the bedroom that he shared with Myles, an eight-year old boy, also orphaned. He was sent from the room just a few seconds before.

Why did my parents have to leave me in this hell? WHY'D THEY HAVE TO DIE IN THAT CAR ACCIDENT! There is no GOD! Lucian sat on the floor, toes curled, fingers balled up into fists, teeth clenched and he looked up at

Owen. Owen screamed when he saw what Lucian couldn't.

Owen ran from the room screaming, "He's the devil! The boy's a devil!"

Lucian got up and looked in the mirror and his eyes were glowing a riveting red. He attempted to calm himself down, like he always read in comic books. "When somebody exhibits abnormal, supernatural symptoms, if they calm down, the symptoms should stop," he muttered to himself. He closed his eyes and took a few deep breaths, counting to ten. In. Out. In. Out. In—his eyes snapped open, still glowing red.

He began floating off of the ground and was thrown directly through the only window in the room, sending shards of glass clattering to the pavement below him. He hovered for a few seconds and then began to rapidly climb into the sky until he was high in the late afternoon clouds. He flew higher and higher, spinning around until the house was a small speck below him. He continued to fly higher even *after* he broke through the earth's atmosphere and was in outer space. He weaved his way between planets, uncontrollably.

He flew for what felt like two hours until he neared his destination. He was at the point where he couldn't even be scared. Anywhere was better than where he was, even if that's millions of kilometers away.

Lucian felt himself speeding up but at the same time, he felt his face being *ripped* apart. He felt as if he was being broken down, *atom* by *atom*. The last thing that he saw was a giant glowing *rainbow.*

He woke up in the woods but he didn't feel *tethered.* It didn't feel like he was even on *earth.* In front of him, three beams of light dropped down, surrounding him. He noticed that he had a light-red aura covering his skin.

The first beam was scarlet red, the second was dark, almost blood red and the third was such a light shade of red, it could've been mistaken for pink. They were so bright, he had to shield his eyes. The lights died down and there were two men and one woman standing in their places.

"Lucian Lieber," the first man called. He was white-skinned but old and wrinkled with long white hair and a long, full beard. "I am known as the entity of energy, along with me are time—" he gestured to the elderly women "—and space," he pointed to the elderly black man with a smaller beard and shorter white hair.

"You have been bestowed with our abilities of the manipulation and full authority over time, space and energy," the woman announced.

Lucian nodded viciously, not fully understanding who they were or what they were saying. They all raised their arms and aimed beams of their respective colour at Lucian, transferring their abilities into him. He screamed out in pain.

"You have been chosen, *Lucian Lieber*! Do NOT fail!" the white man bellowed. He then walked up to Lucian, kissed his forehead and quietly whispered, "I'm sorry I left you, son. Everything has a reason. You'll see soon enough."

"Dad?" Lucian asked, confused as the man stepped back. Before anything else could happen the three beams of light exploded outwards, leaving only faint shadows of the trio that was previously there and then Lucian blacked out.

3. <u>CIRCE</u>

Jasmine was out at the mall with her friends until she got a call from her foster-mom, Sarah Kirkman. "Where are you? I'm here to pick you up!"

"Crap," she muttered. "I'm...uh...just talking to the instructor, come inside." Fifteen minute walk, three minute flight. Jasmine left her friends and went around to the back of the mall before she propelled herself through the air and back to the dance studio, where she was supposed to be taking classes. Since she discovered her abilities, Jasmine could move objects with her mind, fly and hear other people's thoughts.

When she got there, Sarah was talking to her dance instructor. "—eighth dance class that Jasmine has missed in a row. One more missed class and she's out of here. Without a refund."

"I understand," Jasmines foster-mom grunted with a scowl. *Little brat can't stay put, wasting my money,* she thought to herself without knowing that Jasmine was listening in with her telepathy. *It's a good thing, we're giving her back tonight.*

Jasmine had the hint of a smirk on her face but quickly hid it. She always bounced from foster family to foster family. She didn't even know who her real parents were, or where she got her powers from and didn't really want to find out, actually. The powers made her life easier, and she didn't want to make it more complicated than it needed to be.

Jasmine and Sarah walked out of the building, the sun burning hot on her light, almost cream coloured skin. "We're taking you back to your foster home tonight," Sarah proudly announced.

"Oh," Jasmine replied and continued walking as if nothing had been said.

I can't deal with these older kids, I can't wait to tell Carl about the new baby, Sarah thought to herself while slowly placing a hand on her stomach. Jasmine listened in *and put on her infamous devious smirk.*

When they got back to the Kirkman's house Carl asked, "How was it?"

"Um, let's see," Jasmine began to list things on her fingers. "I'm going back to my foster home. I'm out of dance classes. I hate you both and...Oh, yeah! Your wife's pregnant," Jasmine replied walking right back out the door leaving the Kirkmans speechless.

Jasmine went to the park down the street. She watched the younger kids play for a while and then leaped into the sky for an evening flight around her hometown of Toronto, Ontario, and then back home. Within five minutes of getting back, she was already packed and ready to go. It was easier to run away or leave when you only have to carry one backpack.

Jasmine was back at the foster home sooner than she thought possible. They definitely flew way over the speed limit on the drive there, probably just a precaution in case she had more information or secrets to tell.

Before she had even fully walked in, the Kirkmans had signed all of the papers and documents and then Sarah put her arms out, trying to give Jasmine a hug. Out of pity, Jasmine noticed. She simply turned around and walked away without saying a word to either of them.

As she walked back into the familiar place, smelling the familiar scent of leather, she listened to the thoughts of the people she was passing and it made her even happier.

There's the blonde beauty! I knew she'd be back!

Oh great, her again! No one ever wants to keep her.

Great! It's Jasmine!

Damn, she is so hot!

"It is...great to be back!" she joyfully sang to herself. She didn't necessarily love the foster home but it was better than 90% of the people that tried to adopt her.

All that Jasmine knew about her parents was that they probably had powers themselves or conducted some extremely illegal experiments on her. It occasionally occurred to her that maybe she was just...special. She always liked to believe that her parents were heroes—superheroes, but there was always a chance that they were villains too. They left her at this place when she was just a baby. She also pondered that one of them had died and the other couldn't handle—or didn't want—a new addition to the family.

Jasmine got all settled in and gradually fell asleep in the bed that she knew all too well.

4.   <u>TITAN</u>

"You have *four* options," Arthur started. "If your powers develop," he listed them, putting up one finger for each option. "You can give away your powers."

Arion already began to protest but his dad held up a hand, "Let me finish." He put up another finger, "You can live with your powers, save people occasionally but you work for yourself on your own schedule. Third, you can become a part-time superhero, being called in and paid when needed. Fourth, you can become a full-time superhero, getting paid full time."

"Whoa! Back up!" Arion nearly yelled. "I get *paid* to be a superhero?

"Only if you choose to work for the government."

"Did you...?"

"You really think I made as much money as I did by selling my books?" Arthur motioned around with his hands, showing all the technology that he had to buy just in the lair alone.

"I want to do full-time! Think we can talk to them now?"

"Well first, you need your powers, don't you? Now, they should be a reflex." His dad quickly pushed a button on the wall of the dining room and one of the panels from the ceiling above Arion dropped on top of him. Arion pushed his hands upwards and the solid steel panel cracked into two halves against his palms. "Told you," his dad gloated with a smirk.

"HOLY CRAP!" he exclaimed, backing away from the panel as it clattered to the floor. "That could've flattened me!" he yelled, examining his unscathed hands.

"But it didn't. When I left earlier, the tests that I ran were on *you.* I scanned you, your body temperatures, your skins' durability, your strength and weight from each floor panel that you stepped on."

"Wow...sneaky. What powers do I get?"

"Well, to be honest...I don't know. Probably the classic, flight, strength, invulnerability, senses, speed, etcetera. Your powers won't be at their strongest though. There'll be a lot of knock outs and a lot of pain."

"Why are they all over the place?" Arion asked. His dad cocked his eyebrow. "I see no connection between flight, super strength and everything else that I may or may not get."

"It's all manipulated by an invisible force field that lifts you and helps you lift other objects and protects people when you move at high speeds with them or causes bullets to bounce off your skin." When Arion didn't answer, his dad admitted, "It took me a while to understand it all too."

"Interesting," Arion murmured. "I'll race you to the combat room!" he blurted before darting off, the world morphing into a blur around him.

"No flying, ever!" Arion shivered at just the thought. They had arrived in the combat room. Arion was terrified of heights, and he always had been for as long as he could remember. Never went on the monkey bars when he was younger, never been on a plane, he couldn't even sleep on a bunk bed without getting lightheaded.

"Not yet, just stick to the ground for now," his dad agreed.

Arion nodded, "Okay, let's start this."

His dad taught him how to be conscious with his speed and use his *Accelerated Vision*. Arthur stood behind a wall made entirely out of glass while Arion stood on the other side of the glass, in a huge white room. His dad began to work his magic on the control panel. A variety of items were thrown in Arion's direction and he blocked what he could and dodged what he couldn't. There were baseballs, tennis balls, soccer balls, engines and other unexpected items.

His dad called in a few sparring robots to fight Arion. He had already been in self-defense classes for a few years before that and he easily remembered everything. The robots were humanoid. The only difference was that they were like living, moving mannequins with a metallic-silver look. Arion easily took them out and shouted, "Is that all you've got!?" He realized his mistake when more than 20 robots poured into the room.

Arion defeated a couple but was quickly over-come, before he was beaten too badly his dad recalled them and announced into the speaker, "I believe that it's time for a costume. You're going to need something to show if you want the government to take you seriously."

"So, bright coloured spandex is going to make them trust me more? Interesting."

His dad ignored him. "Let's go see Ollie, tomorrow morning. Get some rest, we're getting up early."

"Ollie Wilkinson?" Arthur nodded. "As in, Ollie that I've known all my life? Ollie, your best friend Ollie?"

"Yes! Now stop saying Ollie!" They walked into the elevator. "Wait! Let me show you the quick way to get in or out of here. Here's the remote that opens the hatch doors and you can just go straight out. The elevator is to get in when you're inside the house. Also, see if you can find some more heroes."

"I...I thought there *weren't* anymore," Arion said.

"They're out there," his dad said. "They just need a real reason to come out. Teams help you get in better with the government." Arion smiled and then went to bed with that same smile on his face.

5. QUANTUM

Lucian sat up quickly in his bed, back at the group home, dazed yet still recalling everything from what he *believed* to be a dream. There was a cold breeze coming from his open window. When he turned to look at it, it was shattered to pieces. Shards of glass were scattered all over the floor.

"Maybe a...bird flew into it," he tried to tell himself. He went down the stairs, awake before anyone else and got some cereal from the kitchen. Owen stepped into the room but quickly spun around on his heels, nearly running out of the room.

"Weird," Lucian whispered.

Think of anything you want to eat, he heard in his head. *You control your own reality. Think of the taste and the texture and the shape.*

His mouth began to water as he started thinking about a sizzling pan of bacon while also trying to place the voice, he knew that he had heard it before.

He looked back at the cereal box in his hand and realized that it had changed. In his hand, he was holding a pan of freshly cooked bacon, still sizzling. He looked at his old, white shirt and imagined that it may work the same way. He concentrated on it changing into a nice, brand new red sweater and when he opened his eyes, he was wearing it.

Only then did he place the voice. It was the guy, from his dream...or maybe it wasn't a dream. Lucian finished eating and left the pan in the sink, only to be caught by a different person. It was Owen's wife, Helga. She was surprisingly bigger than Owen was.

"I heard Owen talking to you last night! 'Bout you and your devilish antics! What'd you DO!?" She grabbed his arm and when he tried to escape she raised her hand to slap him. *It is your emotions that fuel your abilities. Pain, sadness and anger create time.*

"How many times must we tell y—" but she stopped. Not just her though, *time* stopped. Helga was stopped in mid-strike, mid-yell and she began to rewind, like a DVD. Lucian backed up until he bumped into the sink. He watched all of the dishes float back to their places in the cupboard by themselves. But then it all stopped abruptly and time began to flow normally. Lucian ran upstairs, terrified.

"What on earth is happening to me?" he asked himself as he flopped onto his bed. Lucian had always been fascinated by superheroes and superpowers. Although he was only five when the heroes disappeared, he felt like it had left an impact on him the most. It meant so much to him to see heroes flying above him, and doing extraordinary things.

Lucian stood up and faced his bed. He concentrated on his blanket and exclaimed, "Frisbee!" The blanket glowed bright red and then began to shrink.

In a few seconds, it had morphed into a scarlet red Frisbee and then all the excess atoms of the blanket that weren't put into the Frisbee were sucked into his body and he suddenly felt full, as if he had just eaten a 4-course-meal.

You can manipulate objects on a subatomic level, allowing you to create new objects as you desire. You could turn a book into an apple, which tastes like beef. You also have the manipulation of time and space, the voice said, as blandly as possible. *You are within the top class of super humans left in your world. The leftover atoms are sucked into your body and replenish sleep, hunger and other physical needs.*

"Whoa," Lucian hollered out loud, not realizing that his roommate was still sleeping.

He heard him shifting in his sleep. Myles rolled over and looked over at Lucian. "What?"

"Nothing," Lucian quickly replied. "Just, feeling...different."

"Well feel different somewhere else!" Myles grunted. "I'm trying to sleep!"

"Whatever," Lucian scoffed, leaving. When he got outside, he thought to himself, *Maybe I'll go for a little, flight around town. Shouldn't be that hard to learn.*

He concentrated on flying high, through the clouds and began to lift off of the ground, straight up, soaring into the morning sky.

6.   CIRCE

Jasmine flew into downtown Toronto in the morning and went on a huge shopping spree with the money that she had borrowed from the Kirkmans. The foster-home that she was in wasn't very strict and she could do nearly anything she wanted on the weekends as long as she was back by 10:00p.m.

Jasmine went to dozens of stores, purchasing loads of clothes. The last store that she went to was weird. It was called Heroesworth and she had never heard of it before. The store had the weirdest clothes, based off of superhero and science-fictional fashion. All of their clothes were either tight, cute or both—two things that she always looked for whenever she was buying clothes.

She purchased a pair of knee-high, red boots along with an electric violet pair of tight *pants and a* tight *electric violet shirt with a zipper. The last thing that she picked up was a small, red domino mask, just barely covering her cheekbones. She changed into them right there in the store after she bought them and left to show off her new outfit. As soon as she stepped outside, she was greeted with the booming sounds of explosions and screaming.*

She looked around and saw smoke burrowing up from about a block down. She reached in her bag and fastened the mask onto her face. She ran over to where the smoke was coming from and saw a teenage girl, maybe 15 or 16 standing in front of a bank across the street with its walls blown off; her skin was a dark shade of brown and she had short black hair that curled over the right side of her face.

There was a huge bald man with her, his skin was a light grey and very rocky with red, lava-like lines flowing through his cracked skin. He had huge, *red demonic wings on his back, spanning at* least *six-feet each with the same look and texture as the rest of him. They walked into the bank and began filling duffel bags with money.*

Jasmine wasted no time and flew further inside. She may be the world's greatest rebel—according to herself—but she's not the type of girl who watches when she can help. She never liked bullies in school, people used to make fun of her all of the time. She shook the thought out of her head and continued on.

The duo was already inside the vault so Jasmine floated in, crossed her arms and joyfully interrupted them by saying, "What's up!?" the monster and the girl turned around to look at her. "Playing dress-up?" she asked referring to their costumes. The muscular monster had a dark red—seemingly leather—X on his chest with a bright red jewel in the center and dark red shorts.

"You're one to talk?" the girl snorted. She wasn't wearing a mask but she had a leather suit with two shades of green, lime and olive. There was a diamond in the middle of her chest, perfectly cut out to show a lot of skin. She wore black tights and lime green boots that went up just passed her shins. She had a thin African accent when she spoke, but by her tone, you could tell she had lived in an English-speaking

country for a while. "The name's *Huntress*, the big guy is *Rage*. Who are you?"

"Uh," Jasmine stuttered. "I don't know yet, first day on the job, but I *do* know that you're not leaving here with *that* money."

"Says who?" grunted Rage. His voice was deep and rugged. Jasmine lowered herself onto the ground.

"Me," she announced proudly, walking towards them. She gave them her devious, *I'm going to crush you* smirk.

"Do you know why I'm called Huntress?" she asked Jasmine.

"Obviously not, I just met you like, two minutes ago, re- member?"

Huntress ignored her sarcasm and continued stalking towards her, "I'm called Huntress because I can take on the trait of *any* animal in the world without my body changing its form or shape. I am literally a human tracking machine and *huntress*. I can use the speed of a cheetah," Her eyes flashed orange and she disappeared in a blur, reappearing behind Jasmine, forcing her to spin around. She didn't like this posi-

tion, she didn't know who to keep her back to, Rage or Huntress. "I could mimic the wall-crawling abilities of a spider," she demonstrated by her eyes glowing again and jumping on the wall, scaling it until she was near the ceiling, "or even the venom of a viper!"

Huntress spat a baseball-sized wad of yellowish-coloured venom directly at Jasmine. Jasmine weaved through the air, back flipping—with the help of her telekinesis—to dodge the venom. Staying in mid-air, she reached out to Huntress telekinetically and pulled her down to the ground, hard. Before Rage could react, a blur of blue, black and red flashed by her and slammed straight into him, spraying colourful bills all over the place.

7.   TITAN

Arion's dad had called Ollie and told him about his power discovery so he stayed up all night making three costumes, and they were going to let him pick which one he liked the most.

Arion and his dad drove to Ollie's shop in downtown Brampton. When they got there his dad lead him to a back room of the tiny

GIFTED

shop. He typed in a passcode on a digitized number pad beside a backdoor. *102299* was the combination, again, Arion noted.

"Knock, knock!" his dad called down the metal stairs. There were tons of boxes lined up against every wall leaving 5 tables in a huge open space, two sewing machines on each. Ollie had his head propped onto his arms, sleeping on the table.

"Toronto...Guardian," he murmured to himself.

"Ollie!" his dad called.

He jolted awake. "What? Huh? Who?" he jumped up and quickly struck his best fighting pose.

Arion and his dad burst out laughing. Ollie scratched his white chin with the stubble of a blond beard. He had hazel-coloured eyes and a huge, bulbous nose.

Ollie turned, looked at the Zimmerman's and slowly lowered his hands. "You were rambling again," Arion's dad told him.

"Sorry," he apologized, "seems like my ability's been..." he trailed off. "Never mind, the costumes?"

"Yes, please," his dad said with a nod.

"Right this way," Ollie led the way to a wooden, floor-to- ceiling

~ 31 ~

wardrobe.

Once they got to the wardrobe Ollie opened the doors revealing a huge room with bright white lights. The costumes were hanging up in the center of the room. They climbed into the wardrobe.

"I haven't made a suit in ten years, I hope they're what you're looking for. I reinforced the suits with the strongest, stretchable materials on earth that your parents and I—personally, mind you—found."

"Wow." The first suit was a plain blue long-sleeve with a small star on the left side of the chest, with white pants and red boots. The second had the star in the center of the chest and, the shirt was dark red, with a red hood attached. The mannequin was wearing a small domino mask that was blue. It had white slips over the eyes that would protect his identity a bit more and the pants were black.

"I tried to incorporate the best of your mom's costume and the best of your dad's into this last one."

Arion's eyes lit up as soon as he studied the third suit. It had a metallic shine to it and was mostly red and blue. It had black highlights under the arms and was perfected exactly to Arion's liking, the emblem was a circle split in half, one side was designed like a red sun and the other was a blue moon. The cape was red with a black border around that and an extra blue border around that. The gloves were red with blue straps, as were the boots. The belt had a red star on the buckle and was blue and black.

Arion immediately reached for the last suit but Ollie quickly slapped his hand. "You get the cape when you can *fly*. It's an unspoken superhero rule! Choose between the two," he barked pointing to the first suits. Arion sighed and chose the one with the star in the center, hood and domino mask. "Don't worry! The hood has wind resistance. It won't fall when you're speeding around."

His dad and Ollie began to have some drinks and turn on the TV as Arion got comfortable in his new suit. The news was on and was reporting a bank robbery, supposedly committed by superhumans in *downtown Toronto*. Arion pulled on the hood and put the mask on.

"I thought the superhumans were gone!" Ollie cried out.

"No," his dad said, "Not gone. We shut them down as best as we could but *these* guys...these guys are new." His eyes shifted to Arion. "Don't even think about it."

"Never do," he said, appearing at the bank in a minute or two.

He saw the commotion and just as the villains began to oppose the *extremely* beautiful super heroine. Arion plowed straight into the huge, eight-foot tall, gray monster, slamming it straight into a stack of bills. Arion jumped up and punched it square in the jaw. If it had felt anything, it sure as hell didn't show it.

"I'm Rage, and who are you?" he asked. "Baby-Atlas? His Mini-me?"

There was a brief shift in Rages facial expression when Arion replied, "No actually, I'm his son, Titan." Arion locked his arms together and swung them around delivering a supercharged blow to Rages face which sent him flying back a few meters.

Arion delivered blow after blow but Rage stood his ground or countered the attacks easily. Rage landed a nice backhand in Arion's face and he flew back, directly into the hero-girl.

"Huntress!" Rage called, "we're out! We've got more than enough money for Suarez!" Both of the heroes watched as Huntress took off and Rage unfolded his huge, dark-red wings, following. Until a bright red blast from the sky knocked them both back down.

8.   <u>QUANTUM</u>

Lucian flew from the group home in Brampton down to Toronto. He saw a fight going on in a bank between two seemingly bad people and two seemingly good people. It was fairly easy to tell the difference because of the colours of their costumes, dark vs. light.

They knocked the (probably) good guys down and tried to fly away but a concentrated blast of energy shot out from Lucian's hands—something that he didn't know that he could do—and it knocked them out of the sky and back to the ground.

He used his ability to manipulate atoms to create a costume for himself. It consisted of a dark red, metal mask with a visor and a dark red cape. The full costume was made with scarlet red and a little bit of white. There were glowing red lines connecting to each other creating an odd pattern that actually looked good. The last thing that he added was a white circle with a blue and red atom in the center. After it was complete he swooped down to help save the day.

Lucian landed and looked for the villains, seeing the two heroes recovering and the monster screaming into the air, "*PIXIE!* WE NEED BACKUP!"

Just then a small person—no larger than your average smartphone—was flying down towards them with small, insect-like wings. By then, the other heroes had gotten up and stood at Lucian's side.

The *Pixie* flew at him and he fired a couple of energy blasts. She easily dodged and began to grow until she became at least twenty-five feet tall. She had short-cropped blonde hair and small features, no older than fourteen. She was wearing white boots that went up to her thighs, a blue lace-up shirt, long blue gloves and an *extremely* short blue skirt. She kicked him directly in his chest and he flew through the front of the bank, smashing into a police cruiser outside.

Five or six policemen immediately pulled out their

guns and aimed for him while the ERT—Emergency Response Team—drove up and did the same. "I'm the good guy!" he called out. "I'm helpi—" he was interrupted by the *not-so-small-Pixie* crashing through the front of the bank. Lucian shot another energy blast into her face and she stumbled but quickly regained her balance.

Lucian flew up into the air—hoping that the police wouldn't shoot him—and shot a couple blasts to her body and chest but she swatted him to the ground like a fly sending chunks of pavement flying up. "Good to know I'm pretty durable too," he muttered to himself. The other heroes seemed to be holding their own against the villains.

He shot three blasts at once, counting on his arcade game skills to help him aim them right. He got one in each eye and one in the middle of her forehead and they exploded on contact. She stumbled and then fell, landing hard on her head. She began to shrink, unconsciously, to her normal size.

The monster leaped at the male hero, but he swung his

arm and back-handed the giant towards Lucian but he was prepared. He pulled his hands together creating a pulse of energy in between them and when the monster was close enough he let it out. It knocked the beast into the wall beside the hero and he was knocked out *cold*.

The hero restrained the monster with a lot of bent metal and the heroine knocked the other villain girl out too. The hero walked up to the crowd that had gathered. "I'm Titan, son of Atlas and Marvella," some people gasped and started to murmur. He continued, "I'm here to continue what my parents started all those years ago and I intend to do my best to protect the world."

He gestured towards Lucian and the girl. "I'm putting a team together. A team that can help the world where the world's human forces can't. As you can see, new villains are coming. I want you two to join my team."

"Is it *The Titans*?" a reporter demanded. "Are you keeping your parents' legacies going?"

"I think that calling themselves *Titans* didn't show that

they were here to help. It made them look like *superiors*, like gods among men.

"I want the public to know *who* we are and *what* we do. We'll be *guardians* to the public. *The Guardians* actually." He looked to Lucian and the girl and flashed a brilliant smile. "What do you guys think?"

Lucian and the girl both looked at each other and simultaneously decided. "I'm in!" which caused the crowd to cheer louder than Lucian had ever heard a crowd cheer before.

9.   CIRCE

After they had helped the police take custody of the villains in separate paddy wagons, Jasmine thought about what she had just done, joined a superhero team with the world's new bunch of heroes. She had the powers, she had the costume, now all she needed was a name. When Jasmine got back to the foster home, after dealing with the police, media and scheduling a rendezvous with the boys, she turned on the news and saw her, Titan and the other guy plastered all over.

"—three super powered teenagers have taken down three super powered villains during their attempt at a bank heist. They call themselves *The Guardians*. This new hero, *Titan*, is the son of the world's greatest known superheroes, Atlas and Marvella, from just over ten years ago.

"Titan has been seen here," it switched to footage of the bank fight, "along with two other unnamed heroes."

She changed the channel and a man, seemingly homeless, appeared, "They're freaks of nature!" he yelled. "We know for sure that the Titan kid isn't human, what about the other two? Are we really going to put the world's fate and trust in the hands of *kids* with fancy costumes?"

Jasmine switched off the TV and muttered to herself, "Barely even one hour and we're already getting hate."

But then a thought occurred to her. *What if I'm not human...* she quickly shook the thought from her head. *Let's cross that bridge when we get there.*

She moved to her laptop and searched up *Magical Names*. On the first two websites she saw the names Jasmine and Crystal, apparently, the two most magical names in the *world. But then she saw a name that she loved: Circe*

"That sounds like the perfect name for you," a male voice declared behind her. She whirled around and pinned the man to the wall of her room telekinetically with a loud thud. The man continued to talk as if nothing had happened, "Circe was a goddess in some stories, in others a sorceress but usually a protector of people. It's perfect because you think of yourself as a goddess and you are a sorceress and currently have an attraction to protecting people."

"What the hell do you know about me?" Jasmine demanded. She flung up her hands and he slammed against the ceiling. "You know nothing about me! Who are you!?"

*"I'm Edward Roland, your father," he began. "I was born in the year 1422 in England. I was cursed by a sorceress. The curse was to fall in love with every sorceress I met, but I was **gifted** with the great abilities of immortality, telepathy, telekinesis and teleportation. That was the good part of the curse, made me feel powerful...superior," he raised his hand and dropped from the ceiling, completely negating Jasmines powers. "The immortality just increased the amount of sorceresses that I could meet by the tenfold." His hair was*

short and bright blond, spiked upwards and his eyes had a slight purple glow to it. *Just like mine,* she thought.

"Around 16 years ago," he continued. "I met your mother. She was a sorceress, very powerful, the best I've ever met and I've lived for over 5,000 years. I became known as *Immortales* and your mother was known as *Hecate,* and we both decided to become *superheroes.* It was the... *hip* thing back then, I guess you would say. Then you came along and everything was great. But then, that so-called *hero* that they called Atlas took her away from us." he was sad, she could sense it through her telepathy.

"You are your mother's daughter," he joked. "But you are also your fathers' daughter. Your psychic abilities are great, very powerful, but I've had centuries to practice, you've had a few *years.*"

"I know you!" she croaked, her eyes widening. She thought back to when she was a little girl. The *first* night that she stayed at that foster home. The day that the superheroes had disappeared. On the TV, they showed a picture of this man. "You killed Marvella! You destroyed the superheroes! Made them all disappear!?"

"I did what I had to! He took away my wife, so I took away his. Only I also took his job and what he loved doing. If only I had gotten to his offspring too before his powers emerged—"

"Get out!" she cried. "I don't ever want to see you again! Stay away from me. Stay. Out. Of. My. Life!" she yelled sending out a blast of telekinetic energy, causing him to stumble. "I've gone on without you for this long, why not go for another 8,000 years?"

"Is somebody in love?" he asked mockingly. Her face immediately turned red but she wasn't sure if it was from anger or embarrassment. She didn't realize how powerful of a telepath he could be. He was poking around deep, getting into her emotions. "You either stand with me, by my side or against me, where I shall crush you and your friends. Do not cross me, Jasmine. I only want what's best for you."

He disappeared in a flash of purple light. All this time she had thought about her parents, who they were, if they missed her...but no! Her mom's dead and her dad is a superpowered psychopath. She turned around and saw a huge book on her bed. Practice your sorcery, you'll need it if you want to oppose me, he sent into her mind telepathically

The book had a pentacle-star in the center with mysterious markings around it. When she touched the book the markings moved around and spelled out *Hecate's Guide to Sorcery.* She opened the book and read the first lines out loud. *"Only a daughter of Hecate may wield the book of sorcery.* **Venefici potest tantum tenent librum sortilegi.***"*

The book flashed purple immersing her in bright light and she heard millions of words from different languages buzzing around her mind. The last thing she saw was the giant image of a woman looking down at her. Then everything went black.

CHAPTER II: RECRUITS

10.   TITAN

Arion reached Ollie's shop within a few minutes and typed in the passcode to go downstairs. Once he got to the bottom of the staircase, his dad greeted him with a huge bear hug and congratulated him for taking out his first villains and making his team. Villains weren't supposed to be around though, they all disappeared with the heroes, and everyone knew that, so Arion continued to wonder where those guys came from.

Before Arion even knew it he was on his way to the rendezvous point a few hours later. They were set to meet in the *Okanagan Desert, British Columbia.* Around the north side was *Area 52: Superhero District.*

Arion was there in fifteen minutes, give or take a few, cruising and carrying his dad on his back. When they got there he slid his dad off as gently as possible.

"Man," his dad remarked, cracking his back, "I haven't moved that fast in ten years." Arion laughed and they waited for the other two to come.

A couple of minutes later, the energy guy swooped down and landed next to them. "Hi," he beamed, extending his hand, "I'm *Lucian Lieber* but I'm going by *Quantum*, Master of Manipulation. I can control Energy. Time and Space too but to a lesser extent. I love the team name... and your name! Honouring your dads' old team...pure genius!"

Arion and his dad both shook Lucian's hand. Since he was completely covered during the fight, this was the first time that Arion was getting a good look at him. Lucian was maybe 5-foot-10 and had blond hair and red eyes that almost *glowed* in the light.

"Oh my *Gods!*" he whispered as he shook Arthur's hand. Arion raised an eyebrow. "You must be *Atlas!* I'm a big fan, sir and I appreciate everything that you've done for this country—world, actually. I have every single one of your comics and movies and novels and...well...can I have your autograph?"

"Maybe later, Lucian," his dad promised with a laugh.

"Now we just need to wait for——" Arion began.

"Me?" Jasmine asked, dropping down beside them.

"It's amazing what you can do with telekinesis!" Lucian quietly whispered to himself. "I think I have it too...kind of...maybe." Lucian turned and started muttering to himself.

"Anyway, I'm *Jasmine...Roland.*" She seemed to wince at her last name as if it was new to her too and Arthur's smile faded as she went on. "I'm a telekinetic, telepathic, I can teleport...supposedly, and I'm a sorceress. I'm kind of liking the name *Circe...*"

After that little meet-and-greet, Arion's dad led them underground, eyeing Jasmine closely.

When they got into the underground facility they saw so much stuff that they probably shouldn't have. There were test tubes with growing things inside of them and animals living inside and bunches of other gene-splicing things too with scientists taking notes. They——hopefully——paid no attention to the heroes. Every security guard took *one* look at Arion's dad and quickly turned their heads, looking the other way. Some even whistled. As soon as they stepped in each room a wall shot up behind them, closing them off from the last.

After walking through a few rooms, they finally got to the room that Arthur wanted them to be in. There was a man with short salt and pepper hair and a silver goatee yelling at a bunch of geeky looking workers once they arrived to the control room. "I WANT YOU TO FIND THOSE KIDS FOR ME! ALL SIX OF THEM! I. Want. Them. Here. YESTERDAY!"

"But sir," one of the workers stuttered, "we haven't perfected time-travel yet. Maybe with a few more years——"

"IT WAS AN EXPRESSION!" he bellowed. "Cross reference all of the information that we've gathered with the superhumans we have on file!" The worker scurried away and Arion's dad coughed behind him. "What now?" he grumbled.

"Atlas!" he exclaimed once he saw him. "Err——I mean Arthur. What brings you here with three minors that should not have witnessed half of the things in the previous room?" he craned his neck to look behind them, making sure that the doors were closed. "And where's my security!?"

Arion tapped his foot on the ground impatiently. "Allow me to take care of this, *dad!* Maybe my *flying* friends and I should leave you two alone." Lucian and Jasmine floated behind him as they dramatically left the room.

"I knew it!" the man exclaimed.

His dad sighed, "Sure you did, *Corbin.* I'm surprised this place is still running. Should've been shut down years ago."

"We just do police, firefighters and medical dispatch now. As super heroic as most humans can be. We send 'em all across the country! Technically we're *Area 52: Dispatch Unit.*" Corbin sighed as if he missed having superheroes around. "I jumped at the chance when the Prime Minister—personally, mind you—asked me to track down these new heroes and bring them in, no matter *what* the cost."

"If you're only doing dispatch right now," Lucian began, "what's with all the...um—" he cleared his throat, "—*stuff* in the previous room." Corbin waved away the question as if it were unimportant.

"These kids want to work under your command, they want a team, *The Guardians.*" Arthur looked back at Arion, who nodded, confirming before he continued.

"What are they asking for? Where are their parents?" Corbin demanded, still scanning his computers for leads on the villains.

Arthur continued answering for them, "I'm Arion's...only parent, Jasmine is a foster child—" his dad winced when talking about Jasmine, "—and Lucian is in a group home. They're just looking for a good offer."

"How does $3,500 a week with all benefits, sound?" Corbin asked. "Isn't that what you got paid?"

"Something like that," Arthur muttered.

"So this is where our tax dollars go?" Jasmine asked under her breath. Arion couldn't help but smile.

"Done! We need heroes, now more than ever," he agreed looking at one of the screens showing footage of Huntress, Rage and Pixie. "All supervillains are transported to *our* secure facility, not handed over to the police. You can't even *begin* to comprehend how difficult it is to transfer them out of police custody! Paperwork and overtime and a lot of crap that I *don't* want to deal with. Am I understood?"

"Uh-huh." Arion said. "Anything else?"

"If you want to work here, your team works for me. And that means that you are on *my* team. And as the leader of this team, I strongly suggest that *we* get some more teammates."

11.   <u>QUANTUM</u>

Lucian was amazed that in the timespan of just a few hours he was a becoming a full-fledged superhero. Lucian, Jasmine and Arion were following Corbin and Arion's dad around Area 52. They got a short tour before being brought into a room where three out of the four walls were made out of holographic computer screens.

"You guys can cycle through the files that we have," declared Corbin. "It's not much, but it's what we could find and keep under wraps."

The three kids got to work as his dad and Corbin left. "There's a kid here who can teleport a few hundred feet," Lucian called to them.

"Nah," Arion disagreed. "We need some pretty powerful people, people who can fight with us and not be defeated easily."

"I found a girl, *Meredith Rainwaters*," Jasmine announced, "She has water-based abilities. The government gave her a private island in—" it seemed as though she was calculating something, "—the center of the Atlantic to keep tabs on her."

"Sounds good to me," Arion agreed.

"Me too," Lucian echoed from behind his screen. He saw a girl who could shapeshift, a guy who could control insects...

"Found one!" Arion called out.

"Who is it?" Jasmine asked while reading her printed papers.

"This guy, *Blake Gilbert*, can manipulate light. He's basically *made* out of it. He lives on the coast of *California*."

"Sounds good," Jaz and Lucian agreed after a few seconds of thought.

"I got another, he's full human but he seems pretty cool." Lucian continued, "He's the son of Artemis, the one from *The Titans* and has all of her skills if not *more*, name's *Benito Suarez*."

They printed the papers and Arion changed from civilian clothes into his costume by spinning repeatedly so that he couldn't be seen. "Jaz, get Meredith, Lucian, get Benito, I'll take Blake."

"Wait!" Lucian called after him. "I've been developing this thing for you. I'm sorry if it comes across as creepy, I just love superheroes and, it took me a couple hours but...give me your clothes."

Arion handed him his clothes without any questions. He morphed Arion's clothes into a small button and put in onto the waist of Arion's costume.

"Push it." Arion did as he was told. "Stick out your arms, spread your legs, it takes about two seconds to load." Again, Arion complied.

There was a bright blue disk that expanded around his waist and split up into two separate ones, one moving upwards and the other moving downwards. After the lights dimmed his suit was gone and he was wearing the clothes that he was wearing before.

"Push it again," Lucian instructed, this time examining it.

"Oh my God, how did you do this? We only met a few hours ago," Jasmine gaped, in awe.

"I'm a fast worker. It was pretty simple actually. All that you need to do is rearrange the atomic structure of—"

Jasmine raised her hand. "My brain already hurts," she interrupted.

"You're a genius!" Arion cried.

"I've been told. I also developed these things." He reached into his pocket and pulled out six little blueberry-sized devices. He handed two to each of them and kept two for himself. "Once you put these in your ears, you won't even feel them. They're nearly invisible unless someone thoroughly examines your ear. Tap once to activate speech, tap twice for vibrate, hold to turn off or on and they are completely waterproof, fireproof, hopefully.

They're obviously untested and I used the specs of a

broken cell phone as reference. With my powers I discovered a new spectrum with these sound waves. I found a way to have our signals ride on them, we won't be able to be hacked...I hope."

"I think we found our team genius. We'll start tomorrow," Arion announced. "Everyone just chill and go home, meet back here tomorrow at... say noon, with your recruit and that's it."

The next day, Lucian arrived in Pennsylvania within a few minutes of 11:30. He flew down towards the Suarez' house and knocked on the door. A woman in a wheelchair answered. "Hi, Mrs. Suarez! I'm looking for Benito."

"Um, sure," she mumbled. "*Benny!* **La puerta! Es para ti!**"

"Okay! **Gracias, mami!**" someone yelled from inside. Lucian heard footsteps running down the stairs. The boy came to the door as his mom rolled away. Lucian noticed that he had short brown hair and brown, mocha coloured skin, like his mom. "What happened to your clothes, man? What's with the cape?"

"This may sound weird," Lucian began, "but I know about how your mom was Artemis and how she's been training you. I'm a part of a new superhero team called *The Guardians* and we want you to join us. You'd work for the government, same people that employed your mom."

He set his jaw and looked around as if debating. "I'm not interested."

"But—"

"Listen, you seem like a nice kid but you people are the ones that put my mom in that wheelchair. Do you under-stand me? We don't want anything to do with you heroes anymore! You better get out of here before my dad gets home. *That* won't be pretty."

"Yeah," Lucian said. "Alright." Benito slammed the door in his face.

12.   CIRCE

Jasmine flew across the ocean, searching for the island that Meredith lives on. When she saw it, she almost dropped out of the sky. The island was bigger than a small town and it was all for just one person. The island was nearly a jungle, covered in trees and plants. She landed on the sandy dock and was on Meredith's doorstep after about 10 minutes of searching for it.

"Hi," Jasmine said to the girl who opened the door. She had long black hair and sea blue eyes that were rippling as if they were small pools of water with rocks being dropped inside every few seconds.

"Hi..." She prolonged the word, her coffee-coloured skin, creased around her mouth. She poked her head outside, looking around. "How... did you...um..."

"Get here?" the girl nodded. "I flew."

"In a plane?"

"Nope."

"Helicopter?"

"Nope."

"Ah," she realized. "You must be the girl that they've been talking about on the news along with Titan and that

other boy."

"Yeah, kind of." Jasmine thought for a minute, "I'm Circe, from The Guardians. I know about your abilities and everything. We were wondering if you wanted to join us and consider becoming a member of our team."

"I don't know..."

"You'll be paid $3,500 a week," Jasmine said quickly. "Depending on how fast you can swim, you can stay here and don't have to move. You need to come back with me now though..."

"Okay, but at least stay for a while. I haven't had people here in...well, ever! Besides my private tutors and the people who bring me my drinks. The government takes good care of their oh-so-precious super-powered people. They send drinks here twice a week! Sea water gets really boring."

"But your island is so big," Jasmine told her, smiling. "Wait, you can drink sea water?" she asked as her smile faded.

"I know, maybe a bit too big, and yes, I can live off of sea water. Would you like some tea?"

"That would be great thanks."

Meredith left for about a minute and came back with two cups. "I would offer you some cookies or crackers but I can't eat, so I have nothing edible here, only drinks."

"Oh, that's...different. So, how did you get your powers?"

"Well, all that I know is that I'm fifteen years old. I think that my powers might come from an ancient water spirit-god or something. But my first memory is waking up lying on a sidewalk, two years ago, in British Columbia. All that I could remember was my name, age and feeling drawn to any form of water. Then the agents came and...well they gave me the island. I guess they want to keep me alive or something like that. What about you?"

"My mom was a sorceress, and my dad was a..." she wanted to say, *supposedly dead, wanted criminal, murderous psychopath,* but instead said, *"Super powered human and I just...kinda inherited their abilities."*

"Oh, cool, can you perform any spells?"

*"**Ecomas Demoro**," she spoke and her clothes instantly changed into her superhero costume.*

"Wow!" exclaimed Meredith, backing up on the chair.

"Yeah, I'm still learning but I thought that could come in handy so it was the first one that I learned." Jasmine gulped her tea, despite it being scalding hot. "Ready to go?" she asked.

"Ready as I'll ever be, I guess."

"Put this in your ear," she said tossing her a communicator and giving her the same explanation that Lucian had given her and Arion.

"Alright," she confirmed, after it was adjusted. "You go up top, I'll go down low!" She jumped into a pool behind the couch—that Jasmine hadn't noticed—and resurfaced after a few minutes, changed into a bikini. "This leads to the ocean, I'll meet you outside." She dove under the water, swimming at speeds unseen to the human eye. It was a good thing Jasmine wasn't human. She followed closely behind her, all the way back to shore.

13.   TITAN

Arion ran fast enough to reach the house in ten minutes although he probably could've made it there in two or three.

When he got to the address he was extremely surprised to see a rundown shack/beach-house combination. Arion walked up to the house and knocked on the door, causing it to fall down in a loud crash. "Damn super strength," he muttered to himself. "Hello?" he called out. There was a huge yellow flash and Arion screamed out, feeling a burning sensation behind his eyes.

He tried to open them but realized that they *were* open, but he just couldn't see anything. He started screaming.

"Oh my God, dude. I'm so sorry! Are you okay? Dammit!" The voice was tinted with a metallic, static-like noise. Arion heard it coming from beside him but it was mixed with millions of other sounds. He heard a dog barking and wind rustling some tree branches. He heard the crash of the waves, loud as an explosion, right beside his ear. He heard the wings of a seagull flapping mixed with the sound of a plane soaring, all *directly* beside him.

He couldn't see, but he could *hear* everything. He heard the guy talking again, "I'm sorry. It was just a safety thing, it's never done this to anyone before. It usually dazes them until I can see who they are."

"I CAN'T SEE!" Arion screamed throwing his arms into the air. He felt his arm hit something hard and he heard wood crashing and splitting, just before he blacked out.

When he woke up from his dream he was in a dark room. "Are you okay?" a voice asked. The same voice from his dream.

"Yeah, can you turn the lights on please, it's extremely dark."

"You're in California, and its 11:30, the light is as bright as can be." Arion heard a hint of sarcasm in his voice.

"You mean, that wasn't a dream? I'm blind!?" The guy sighed.

"Yes and I'm sorry!"

"You're sorry!?" Arion tried to sit up but instead fell and hit the floor, hard, sending vibrations up to his ears. "TURN THAT OFF!"

"Turn what off man?" the guy started backing up slowly, creaking the wooden floor. Arion heard the creak as if someone was endlessly sliding their nails down a chalkboard.

"ENOUGH!" Arion screamed and the guy stopped moving. "Who are you?"

"*Blake...Blake Gilbert.*"

"Okay, Blake, why the hell can't I see anything!?"

"I kind of blinded you."

"WHY?"

"It's always just been a small blast, never enough to actually blind someone. Maybe you have sensitive eyes."

"Maybe you just blinded one of the world's newest superheroes!"

"DAMMIT! You're Titan!? I saw you on TV!"

"Really? Hadn't noticed! I only came here to talk to you."

"Me? Why would you want to talk to *me?*"

"I wanted you to join my team! You're one of the only truly super powered people left in the world."

"Oh," Blake whispered. Arion could sense the shame in his voice.

"Yeah, and—" Arion stopped talking and backed up into a corner, being forced to listen to everything around him, trying to focus. He heard a helicopter passing by, and a woman yelling at her kids. He heard it all, everything, at the exact same time.

"What's wrong man?"

"You don't hear that?" he demanded.

"Hear what? I only hear you yelling at me!"

"I'm hearing EVERYTHING!"

"Okay," Blake said, sounding like he was reassuring himself more than Arion. "Just breathe, okay?"

"Okay."

"Just listen to one thing, focus on one thing." While Arion tried to focus on one thing he heard the water from the dripping tap crashing into the sink with loud thunder-like booms.

"I can't!" He took a deep breath. "It's too hard!"

"Focus on my voice! Pretend that it's the only thing there. Isolated, just floating in space. All by itself! Only you can find it. Just focus on all the ups and downs, the tone of it. Focus."

"I got it. I can't hear anything else. Just you."

"Good," Arion heard footsteps leaving and the tap running but it all sounded normal. The footsteps returned and he was handed a glass or cup of some sort.

"Drink." Arion did as he was told and tasted pure crap. He spat it out and dropped the glass.

"What the hell was that?" he demanded Blake.

"Tap-water. All of your senses seem to have been heightened except for your vision. Maybe you just tasted every single particle in the water. We have got to get you to some sort of specialist."

"Just...wait. I'm calling reinforcements." Arion tapped his communicator and sent a message to his team. "Guys, I'm... stuck in California. I need some... help."

"Be there soon!" Lucian replied.

"Same here! Hold on," Jasmine replied.

"They'll be here soon, Blake," Arion assured him. "Just...sit tight."

14.   <u>QUANTUM</u>

Lucian flew as fast as he could. He considered Arion a good friend even though they had just met. He didn't know if that was sad or just plain weird. He was just a few minutes out from the address when a blast of orange fire hit him.

Lucian tumbled out of the sky and landed hard on the sandy beach. He looked down at his singed costume. "YES!"

he heard a guy yell. "I told you they'd work!"

"Suarez's energy signature machine worked too, surprise, surprise!" a girl said.

"Wow...that barely even hurt!" Lucian exclaimed, while pulling atoms from the sand to reconstruct his costume. A stream of blue, arced electricity shot him in his chest sending him skipping across the sand until he slammed into a rack of surfboards.

"I don't have time for this!" he yelled out.

"Yes you do!"

"No I don't!" he yelled.

"Do too!" called another voice.

He turned to see two Asian kids—Japanese, he guessed—maybe around sixteen, standing back to back, arms folded. They were probably twins although one was a boy and one was a girl.

"Who are you guys?"

"I'm Nexus and this is my brother Arc," the girl said. She had long golden hair and bright orange eyes. Arc had a spiked blue Mohawk and lightning blue eyes. They were both wearing armoured body suits, straight out of a comic book with giant robotic gauntlets on their hands.

"Cool names," Lucian scoffed.

Nexus uncrossed her arms and turned to face Lucian. She clenched her fists and blasted two huge waves of fire at him. He raised his hands to block it and a shield of transparent, red-tinted energy erupted from his hands. Arc began to shoot electric blasts at Lucian but they were all being blocked by his new force field. Lucian became confident in his force field and manipulated it as he wrapped it around the twins.

Lucian sealed it tight so that they wouldn't be able to move or use their abilities without burning themselves to a crisp. He lifted it up, flying it behind him on his way to meet up with Arion and Jasmine.

When Lucian arrived at the beach house he walked through the doorway, as there was no longer a door. He leaned the twins inside of the house and continued inside.

"Hello?" he called out. "Titan? You here?"

"Over here!" Arion called.

Lucian ran into the room and saw a glowing yellow guy with a small nose, small ears, (both also glowing), yet no other features. Lucian immediately tackled him, thinking that he was the bad guy. Lucian saw Arion cover his ears once they hit the ground which had caused a small bang.

Lucian swung at the yellow guy but he made a yellow force field just big enough to block Lucian's fist. "Get...*off* of me!" he yelled, blasting Lucian with yellow energy. Lucian was sent flying into the opposite wall.

"Hyperion," Arion said, "stand down!"

"Don't tell me what to do!" yellow guy—Hyperion— yelled.

"You don't want to mess with me," Lucian said, creating balls of glowing red energy in his hands. "I'll *destroy* you!"

"LUCIAN!" Arion yelled. "*Stand DOWN!*" Hyperion's

hands began glowing too, they were yellow. Hyperion and Lucian stood opposite each other, Arion now standing in the middle.

Lucian slowly killed the energy in his hands. "I'm sorry. I think we got off on the wrong foot. I'm Quantum, the king of time, energy and space—"

"King?" Arion asked, raising his eyebrow.

"It has a nice ring to it!" Lucian retorted. He looked back to Hyperion. "I'm assuming you're named after the ancient Greek Titan of light?" He extended his hand to him.

"Don't touch me," Hyperion said, killing the glow in his hands and turning away.

"Blake—" Arion began.

"It's Hyperion," he interrupted. "It sounds cooler."

Lucian took a closer look at Arion. He was standing there, looking through him, as if he didn't even notice that he was there and then he saw his eyes. He had bright, milky white eyes instead of the usual bright blue.

"Arion, are you..." Lucian stammered.

"Yeah, I'm...well, I'm blind," he replied.

Lucian stood there, mouth agape until he heard a voice behind him say, "Who are the two Japanese kids wrapped up against the wall?" Lucian turned to see Jasmine standing next to a *beautiful* girl in a bikini.

15.   <u>CIRCE</u>

"YOU'RE BLIND!?" Jasmine demanded.

"Yep, pretty much," Arion explained as nonchalantly as possible. Arion and Blake—going by Hyperion—had explained the situation to all of them.

"Never mind that though," Arion continued. "We'll get the scientists to look at me back at Area 52. Hyperion said that it's never been permanent and my eyes are just extra sensitive. If my sight isn't back by next week, then I'll start flipping out. Have you guys thought of a name yet, Meredith?"

"Yeah," she replied. She looked at Jasmine who was just freaked out by how cool he was with being blind. "It's—
"

"How about *Aquagirl?*" Lucian asked. "Or *Mera?* Or *Ocean?* Or *Aqua?* Or *Mermaid?* Or *Amphitri*—"

"Shut up!" Jasmine and Meredith both yelled at the same time.

"My name is *Atlantica!*" she called out.

"Alright," Arion said. "*Titan, Quantum, Circe, Atlantica* and *Hyperion?*"

They all nodded. "I can hear you nodding but, I can't see you, remember?" Everybody shifted their weight uneasily, not too sure what to say. "We're going public with these names soon. Are you guys sure that these are what you want?" They all mumbled their agreements. "Well then, I need a ride home."

Jasmine volunteered to take Arion and she floated him next to her, Hyperion teleported away, Lucian and his caught villains flew away and Meredith (who flew on a cloud, since they're made out of water and air.)

"It's a really good thing I can't see or else I'd probably be screaming my head off right now."

"Why?"

"I don't do heights," Arion explained, "at all."

"Oh, want to walk? We're not too far anymore. I haven't tried teleporting yet but..."

"It's alright." Jasmine felt a little bit embarrassed but continued to fly.

They flew in silence for a bit until Jasmine finally asked the question, "What do you see?"

"I don't know, Jaz. It was nothing at first, just blackness and colours, like rubbing your eyes while they're closed. But now I can see a few things, really blurry things."

"Oh," she said, not quite sure how to reply to that.

"Hey, it's progress, right? I was blinded not even an hour ago and my other senses were off the chart."

"Why are you afraid of heights?" she asked him. "Any specific reason?"

"My dad told me that fears were hereditary on my mom's home planet, but the Zonarians were fearless, all their fears overcome in childhood or early adulthood.

"My mom was terrified of heights, that's why she could never fly, never really got the chance to try either," he

paused for a second and took a deep breath. "I guess I inherited her fear and sometime, I'll have to overcome it through some sort of experience. I'm kind of hoping that's soon, but I'm really hoping that it isn't."

They flew in silence for the rest of the way back to Area 52.

After they had gotten there, Jasmine began to think. She would never admit it, and she would kill anyone if they found out, but she really liked Arion. There was something about him that drew her to him. She couldn't decide what it was; his blue eyes, or the power that he had, or just how calm he always is, she just really liked him.

She was walking around the building, when someone came out in front of her. "Ms. Roland," he said. He seemed to have no emotion. He looked like some sort of agent, wearing a suit, tie and sunglasses indoors. "Mr. Corbin would like to have a few words with you."

Jasmine followed the man into the main hallway with office doors everywhere. The hallway was sized for about five people, side by side, so when Lucian and another agent

showed up, there was no problem walking through the hall.
The agents even dropped back to talk to two other agents
who had recently arrived with Meredith and Hyperion.

"What's this about?" asked Hyperion, glowing radi-
antly.

"I have no idea," Jasmine replied, and then the doors to
Corbin's office opened.

16. TITAN

Arion was put to lay down on a steel table in a huge metal la-
boratory. "Mr. Zimmerman, this won't hurt a bit," one of the doctors
told him.

The doctor put something to keep Arion's eyes open and then attempted to push a needle into it. The needle bent against his cornea
and the doctor seemed shocked.

"You're right, it didn't hurt," Arion quipped, sarcastically. "Really,
man?" Arion asked. He blinked, snapping the eye-opener in half and
then he sat up. "Can't you just take a digital, holographic, 3D scan of
my eye balls or something?"

"Uh…" the doctor was speechless. "Yes, I guess that could

work."

Arion shook his head and began to lay down again. The doctor put a bunch of patches and sensors on his face. "Blink twice and then roll your eyes." Arion did as he was told and continued following the instructions that he was being given. Afterwards, the doctor brought up a holographic generation of Arion's eye.

"Your vision is at 20/200. This means that you need to be twenty feet away from something to see what a normal person could see at two-hundred feet."

"Before I couldn't see anything, so it's progress, right?"

"Yes. We have some prototype glasses that we want you to try out. It changes prescription as your vision improves and shifts forms too. You'll be able to see perfectly. Would you like to try them?"

"Yes please," the doctor left the room and Arion used his new super-hearing to focus on what the doctor was saying. "The boy will be fine."

"Are you sure?" asked another voice, his dad's voice.

"I'm sure. Here, you can give him the glasses."

"Thank you, Doctor Martinez."

His dads' footsteps echoed down the hall and back towards the lab. He handed Arion the glasses.

"Doctor Martinez says——"

"I heard what he said."

"How?"

"Blake blinding me…it jumpstarted my senses. My *super* senses."

"All of them?"

"Enhanced hearing, taste and smell, but vision…has yet to come and I don't think touch really counts."

"It manifests as muscle movements. You can do nearly anything with your body, more flexible than the *best* gymnast Looks like something good came out of this after all, son." He reached and put his hand on Arion's shoulder.

"I can hear your hand splitting the air," Arion whispered. "This is so…*cool.*"

"Sorry to burst your bubble but it won't always be cool. I had super hearing too. I had to listen to the cries of thousands of people and *ignore* 99% of them because I had to, look for the one that needed the most attention."

Arion pulled on his new glasses and could see everything perfectly, clear as day. He and his dad strutted out of the room, talking about how they were going to incorporate the new super senses into their training.

17.   QUANTUM

Lucian was in the office with Meredith, Jasmine, Hyperion and Corbin. Corbin sat behind a long wooden desk and the four teens sat in front of that desk in four out of the five chairs.

"Out of my new team," Corbin began, "only *one* out of the five members has a living parent. Therefore, the Canadian government is directly responsible for each and every last one of you.

"You guys can live at this facility or any of our other ones scattered around North America and go to a school or I can get you a house...and you go to a school. I know that you—" he pointed at Jasmine and Lucian "—will be moving up a year in high school soon enough. We'll arrange every-thing for those who are under some sort of protective cus-tody." He looked to Lucian and then to Jasmine, a second time. "Meredith?"

"I want to stay on my island. I can get here pretty fast, I can manipulate the water in a cloud to fly me here."

"Alright, you're free to go then. And work on a cos-tume, for God's sake! A bikini is *not* going to help you fight crime." Meredith rolled her eyes and muttered something about how it might and Lucian couldn't help but smile. Just before she left, Jasmine whispered something to her. She giggled, nodded and then left.

"Blake—"

"I prefer Hyperion now and *only* Hyperion."

"Okay then...Hyperion, I know you can teleport and fly near the speed of light, but I still wanted to give you your options."

"I'll sleep when I'm dead. I don't need a living space."

Corbin nodded. "Okay, then. You're...free to go too,

then!"

"Lucian?" Corbin looked him straight in the eyes. "Do you want to stay?"

"I'll stay, I actually kind of like this place." Jasmine and Corbin both glared at him. "What?" he demanded. "It's growing on me."

Corbin barked a heavy laugh. "Alright, I'll arrange something with your group home to get your belongings sent here. You can choose to either be homeschooled here or you can attend a public school. The year is almost done anyway so we can pick up after the summer.

"Thanks," Lucian said.

Lucian left the room and saw Meredith sitting in the waiting room outside. Before he could say anything she said, "Jasmine asked me to wait for her." He nodded and decided to go for an evening flight, hoping that he wouldn't run into any more baddies on his joyride.

18.   CIRCE

Jasmine was still in the office with Corbin after every-body else had left. She sat there looking at him intently, wait-ing for him to say something.

He let out a small sigh. "And then there were two." When Jasmine didn't say anything he asked, "Where do you want to live?"

"Brampton. Got any places there?" She asked the ques-tion absentmindedly as if she didn't care or mind.

"Yeah, a few."

"I want to go to Kingsbury Secondary School. Any around there?" A hint of a smile played across Corbin's lips.

"Is there something funny?" she asked. "I must've missed the joke."

"You remind me so much of your mother, Jasmine." her ears perked up.

"What do you know about her?" she asked, actually paying attention now.

"Know about her?" He laughed a long, hearty laugh. "She worked for me! I have a file on her, and your dad. I was one of the first to be told when she was pregnant. Her death was...tragic, as was your father's even though he had turned.

Guess he wasn't so *immortal* after all."

Jasmine took three deep breaths, staring at Corbin with wide eyes. "Jesus, kid! You okay?"

"Yeah, I'm fine, just...dizzy," she said shaking her head.

"You, sure?"

"Yeah. What happened to Immortales—my dad? How did you guys kill him?"

"You sure you want to know?" he asked.

"Give it to me as simply as possible," she said, taking a deep breath.

"He was…" Corbin straightened his tie, "decapitated and pulled apart. I don't even have the clearance to know all of the locations but, pieces of his body were scattered at random locations around the world, and off of it as well. We had some pretty good interstellar fliers back in the day—"

"He's back," Jasmine interrupted.

"What?" Corbin looked like he had just seen a ghost. "Are you sure!?"

"He visited me, on Saturday. He followed me home and teleported in, gave me a spell book called, *Hecate's Guide to Sorcery* or something like that."

"Dammit!" he yelled, slamming his hand on the table. "Get out," he said, picking up the phone. "I'll get you your place near your boyfriend." He started punching in numbers on the phone. "Take these and give one to each of your teammates. Explain to them that they work as credit cards and they will be refilled every week and you can get cash instead at any bank. And we distribute new ones if the other is lost— or most likely—destroyed. $10,000 advance, each."

"Um. Okay. Thanks I guess." She took the cards. She tried to read his mind to see what he was thinking but all she got was static and white noise. She gave up and said, "Bye."

When he didn't answer Jasmine stood up, "Um, RUDE!" She left the room without saying another word to him.

Jasmine met up with Meredith in the waiting room. "We got a $10,000 advance, so let's spend it right. Are you with me?" She handed her a card.

"Sure thing, Jasmine."

"I have a feeling we're going to be great, super powered friends. Call me Jaz." Meredith shook her head at the

sight of Jasmines devious smirk.

"I just have to give everyone their cards and then we'll be good to go. Where do you want to go? Paris? Barcelona? I heard about a really nice place in Italy."

"Italy, it is then." Then they took off, using their communicators to call for their teammates.

CHAPTER III: BALLISTIC

19.   TITAN

Arion walked around in the mall, looking for things to buy with his new cash card in his pocket and his new glasses propped up on his nose. They were thin but worked perfectly fine, he could see perfectly fine.

"Arion!" a girl's voice called out. He turned around and rammed right into someone and she fell backwards, landing on her butt.

"Ow! Oh gosh, I'm so sorry," the girl moaned in-between bursts of laughter. "That felt like I just hit a wall!"

"That's alright," Arion assured her, while helping her up. "I've been...uh...working out."

He looked down to see piercing emerald-green eyes staring up at him. "I almost didn't recognize you," she said. "I like the new glasses, it changes your eye colour a bit though."

"If I had a nickel for every time I heard that, *Thalia*, I'd have 5 cents."

She forced a laugh a little bit too hard, and her ivory-coloured cheeks became red. Her black hair bounced with each laugh. *Thalia Garcia* was the most *beautiful* girl that Arion had ever met. She was wearing a short white jean skirt and a blue t-shirt.

Arion and Thalia had been good friends since they had met in the first grade. Thalia was so book-smart that she had been classified as a nerd *before* she was pretty and nothing ever changed. Arion was in the same category, good at a lot of things but always faded into the background.

"I was just walking and I saw you...and I was wondering if you wanted to like go out or something like sometime, like...any-time...not necessarily now or...anything. I'm...going to shut up now..." She started shyly staring at the floor.

Arion pulled up his sleeve and checked his watch. "It's only 6:00," he observed, "the night is still young."

"Cool, now's good."

Arion turned sideways and put his arm out. "Shall we?"

"We shall," she replied as she hooked her arm through his and then they started walking. Arion could *tell* how nervous she was. She was a little bit wobbly and he could hear her heart beating faster than normal. *Cool,* he silently thought to himself.

"Where do you want to go?" Arion asked. They were sitting on the swings in the park, slurping some slushy's from the corner store just down the street.

"Wherever you want to go," Thalia insisted.

"Well I want to go wherever you want to go, so this causes a paradox."

"Nerd," she joked. He smiled, slightly embarrassed.

"How about we just...go see a movie? Those are always good."

"Sure," Thalia giggled, beaming at the idea. *Or maybe she was just beaming at the idea of being alone in a dark room with him,* he thought.

"What do you want to see?" Arion asked?

"Something scary. Like...*Alien Invasion III: Retaliation.*"

Arion shifted his weight. Now that he knew he was an alien, he had no interest in seeing what they fictionalized about them. Although there were probably little green men with big heads and three fingers

on each hand somewhere in the universe, he still didn't like the idea.
"Nah, I haven't seen the first two."

"I'll fill you in."

"I don't know——"

"Please," she begged.

"Sure," he sighed. "There's a showing in 5 minutes. I'll get the tickets."

"Thank you sooo much!" Thalia squealed, she stood on her toes and kissed his cheek, making him the happiest guy in the theatre, for about 20 minutes.

20. <u>QUANTUM</u>

Lucian flew around the Toronto skyline, in costume until he saw Meredith and Jasmine flying up towards him. "Ladies," he said, greeting them with a nod. Meredith seemed to be more focused on keeping her cloud solid than talking to him, he noted.

Jasmine handed him a card. "$10,000 advance," she said also explaining everything else.

"Alright, thanks, and where are you ladies off to on a nice evening like this?"

"Imperia, in Italy. Treating ourselves to a little spoiling," Jasmine sang, waving her new card around.

"This late?"

"It's probably daytime over there," she shrugged.

"Alone? Now you see, I—a kind gentleman—can't let two super-powered girls—such as yourselves—fly all the way to Italy *alone*," Lucian warned. "But if you don't want me to come, that's cool too," He began to lay down on the air, put his chin on his hands and put on a false pout. "I'll just chill over here, by myself."

"Okay," Jasmine said flying away but Meredith pulled her to the side and whispered something to her. "Fine, you can come!"

"YES!" he screamed with a fist pump. "You guys won't even know that I'm here. I'll be like a phantom. Better yet, a ghost. Did you guys know that there are multiple significant differences between the two? You see, phantoms are more like—"

"Oh, yeah. Like he's not even there," Meredith muttered while Lucian kept rambling.

"It was your idea to bring him," Jasmine scoffed.

After listening to Lucian talk nearly non-stop for the past fifteen minutes, as soon as they hit the ocean Meredith said, "I'm out," and dropped off of her cloud into the water.

"TAKE ME WITH YOU!" Jasmine called after her.

By the time they had reached Imperia, Jasmine and Meredith had attempted to kill Lucian three times, once with telekinesis, the other through drowning and the last one, by shark.

"You guys play kind of rough," Lucian said. "Don't you think?"

"Shut up!" Jasmine screamed.

"Okay, baby. Chillax!"

"I am *chill!* And do *not* call me baby!" she hissed.

"Maybe if every once in a while you'd just shut the—" in the middle of her sentence a stream of water erupted from the ocean in between the two.

Meredith floated up on the stream and asked, "Are you two ladies done?"

"She started it!" Lucian yelled.

"Oh, I started it? I will shove my foot sooo far up your—"

"Enough!" Meredith cried, blasting them both with water. "In case you haven't noticed, we have company." She pointed to the streets where wild cats of all different shapes, sizes and types were running up and down the street below them.

"Lions and tigers and..." Lucian stopped and began to think. "HEY! I AM NOT A LADY!"

Meredith shook her head in disbelief and directed her spout towards the commotion with Jasmine right behind her and Lucian grumbling to himself.

21. CIRCE

"CALL FOR BACKUP!" Jasmine screamed at Lucian.

"I'm a little bit busy!" he screamed back. He had a lion laying on top of his chest, jaws open with his hands inside of its mouth, prying it open to keep it from clamping on his face.

"Meredith?" Jasmine asked.

"Cats don't hate water!" she yelled back from some-where behind her. "Go figure!"

She faintly heard Lucian scream, "CIRCE!" as she was attacked by a dozen cats. She stopped and closed her eyes for what felt like 5 minutes. When her eyes snapped open, she cast a purple light throughout the street while unleashing a huge telekinetic blast that sent all of the cats sprawling. She screamed into her communicator, "Hyperion, Titan, we need tons of help right now!"

"I'm kind of on a date…is it that important?" Arion re-plied. Jasmine didn't even respond. She had thought that he liked her. It sure as hell looked like it, but she realized that it was kind of stupid to think so. They had just met.

"I don't care!" she hissed. "If it wasn't important I

wouldn't call you! Get your butts to Imperia, Italy now!"

Hyperion flashed into view and immediately began taking on some lions, blinding them and creating solidified light constructs to fend them off.

Arion blurred in behind them, grumbling something about someone named Thalia, which infuriated Jasmine even more.

"We need a plan, doll!" Hyperion yelled over the roar of the animals.

"Really!?" Meredith demanded. "I hadn't noticed!"

"I got it!" Arion called. "Follow me."

They met up in a park, just down the street from where the cats were running wild throughout the streets. "Meredith," Arion began, "can you create a hole in the ocean, straight down?"

"Yeah. In my sleep."

"Good. Do it! Make it as big as you can! And...um...stay awake," he added. "Circe, go help her. Everyone else, wait for their signal, then I'll tell you what to do."

Jasmine was tempted to defy Arion but whatever problems she had with him outside of battle needed to stay outside of battle. She cleared out with Meredith and they went out to sea, far from the land. Meredith clapped and then spread her hands slowly as if pushing against an unseen force that was keeping her from opening her hands.

Jasmine moved in front of her but kept her distance, using her telekinesis to help. The ocean began to swirl and create a whirlpool, as if the water was being drained out. "Ready!" Meredith told the rest of the team once it was drained enough.

Jasmine saw them coming from kilometers away. There was a humungous cage with thick bars, nearly like a prison cell except it was made out of...light!? Arion was running under it, for extra support, Hyperion was on top of it, concentrating on holding his construct together and Lucian kept a force field around it to help keep the smaller animals from slipping out between the bars and to keep some weight off of Arion.

Jasmine redirected her attention to the whirlpool which was nearly all the way to the floor of the ocean.

She realized that Meredith kept a tidal wave from starting by evaporating the water as she pulled it up into the air.

When Jasmine realized that her services were no longer needed by Meredith, she departed to help the guys until she heard the roar of a chopper above her.

"Here you can see, The Guardians—the superhero team—saving Imperia from dozens, if not hundreds of wild cats!" *she heard someone—a woman—say from the helicopter in Italian as it pulled closer. Jasmine could sense what she was saying from what she was thinking. She remembered everything that she had learned from that overwhelming amount of language from that book of sorcery.*

She gripped the helicopter telekinetically and stopped the blades from spinning. She told them they had to leave before they got hurt in fluent Italian but the newscaster just shoved a microphone and camera in her face and demanded answers.

"I am Circe," *she said in Italian.* **"We are trying to do our job which I cannot do with you here. Therefore you must leave or be escorted out."**

"Jeeze, kid," *the news lady replied,* **"just doing my job."**

"Me too."

The news lady spun her index finger around to tell the pilot to fly off and as Jasmine spun the blades again, they took off.

22. TITAN

Arion was running fast enough to run on water but slow enough to let the others keep up, jogging in place at some points. They were helping a little bit but Arion felt as if he was literally holding the sky. He knew that he was surpassing his weight capacity by lifting this cage, even with the help of the others. Arion simply ran up to the whirlpool while holding the cage and threw it in lightly.

He made the mistake of looking down into the hole and the world immediately warped around him as his fear of heights set in and he fell. He heard Jasmine call his name and then...nothing over the rush of the water as Meredith let it all go and the cage broke.

Arion's glasses were able to morph into the domino mask that he needed for his costume, but even they couldn't stay on through that much water, ripping at his face. He was pulled under and his vision was blurred by his loss of sight and the dark, murky water. He felt the pressure from the water pushing him down and he saw a blurry figure, swimming towards him.

Meredith! He thought to himself. He began to swim up towards her, feet kicking until he felt the clamp of jaws around his body, pulling him deeper into the water.

He knew that he could hold his breath for a long time but whatever that thing was, it had knocked the wind out of him forcing him to push out his breath and suck in a mouthful of water but if felt as if he had just sucked in...air! He could breathe underwater! He thrashed around until his fist connected with the animals' nose, from the feel of it, he assumed that it was a shark. The shark released him and swam away.

He kicked and began swimming away. He heard the shark coming up again and he began kicking his legs, hard. He moved them so fast, that they began moving at super speed, causing a barrage of bubbles and water to push the shark away. He shot out of the water like a torpedo flying several feet into the air. A giant yellow butterfly net shot out under him and caught him, mid-air.

"GET ME DOWN FROM HERE!" he yelled at Hyperion, fear rising

in his voice from being off of the ground. The butterfly net disappeared with a movement of Hyperion's hand and Arion fell to the water. He righted himself mid-air and landed on the water bouncing from foot to foot really quickly to keep from sinking.

"That went..." Lucian started to say.

"Well..." Jasmine supplemented.

"Yeah," he nodded furiously, "that's what I was thinking!"

"Where's Meredith?" Arion asked. As if on cue, her head rose from the water along with the rest of her body, slowly until she was standing on the rippling waves.

"You broke that shark's nose," she muttered.

"Why the hell did it attack me!?"

"He thought you were someone or something else. The lions disappeared after they were drowned, all of them."

"Alright, I'm out." Arion announced, about to take off.

"You might need these!" Meredith tossed him his domino mask which morphed into glasses in mid-air. "You might want to be able to see your date."

"Crap! I forgot all about Thalia!" Jasmine flew up higher and further away from them. "Thanks," he winked, rushing back to the movie theater.

23. QUANTUM

Hyperion teleported back to Area 52, Jasmine had stormed off and Arion ran back to his girlfriend, so that left Lucian and Meredith.

"So…" Meredith said. She was floating on her back in the water, kicking her feet, still moving fast, but not too fast and Lucian flew just a few feet above her.

"So…" Lucian repeated.

"What do you think happened with the lions and tigers and…stuff?" she asked.

"I don't know, can't *you* talk to animals?"

"Only animals that are *related* to water in some way."

"That seems a bit useless, no?"

Meredith stopped and positioned herself to stand on the water. She closed her eyes and raised her arms for about five minutes and then, as if on cue, hundreds of fish, sharks, whales, jellyfish, octopi and other animals that even Lucian—boy genius—didn't recognize, shot out of the water in a funnel at least 50 feet high.

"Useless, huh?"

"That was actually pretty cool."

"Show me something cool," she told him.

"I can turn your clothes into water," he joked, with a hopeful, crooked grin.

"NO!" she screamed dropping back underwater, as if she had that much on in the first place. Lucian took advantage of the chance that she was distracted and firmly planted his lips on hers.

"I like you," Lucian gushed after he had pulled away. "I like you a lot and I don't usually feel this...um...uncomfortable around a girl. Your powers amaze me and you're beautiful and cool and I'd really like to get to know you some more. I'd like to take you out, on a date, to a place that no girl could ever dream of, I *promise* that it'll be spectacular."

Meredith just stared at him. Lucian knew that she barely knew him but was hoping that she'd give it a shot anyways. "I'll tell you what...if you beat me to Area 52...maybe...I'll think about it. She sunk under the water and zoomed off.

He smiled and chased after her. He was keeping up too until a swirling, rainbow portal opened up in front of him, ripping time and space, while also sucking him inside like a vacuum.

24. <u>CIRCE</u>

*Jasmine arrived at Area 52 just after Hyperion. "**Ecomas Demoro**," she chanted, her superhero suit, instantly changing back into civilian clothes.*

"Jasmine!" Corbin yelled from down the hallway.

"Yeah," she muttered in an obnoxiously annoyed tone.

"We found you a place in Brampton, within walking distance of your preferred school," he winked twice, simultaneously saying, "Wink, wink," and nudging her arm with his elbow.

Jasmine felt her face getting hot. "I don't *want* to go to that school anymore!" she cried.

"Too bad, you're already registered and you're in every single one of *his* classes. Cute, huh?"

He handed her a card with the address on it and he barked his laugh, walking away. It took all of her will-power not to clench him telekinetically and whip him into the nearest wall. "And I just changed out of my suit, too," she murmured to herself. She flew off out of the door and into the air while saying, "**Ecomas Demoro**," again.

She arrived at her destination fairly quickly, it was within the hour but, it had taken her a bit to find it. The house was big enough for a family of four but she had it all to herself. She walked into the house and realized that all of her stuff had been sent there, including some new stuff.

She unpacked her things and made her house feel slightly more like a home. The home phone rang throughout the house. Jasmine levitated it to her hand and answered it, "Hello?" she said into the receiver.

"How are you liking the new place?" Corbin asked

through the phone.

"It's okay. Not a home yet but it will be pretty soon."

"Good, it's only a temporary place," he said. The line went dead.

"Um, rude," Jasmine scoffed.

She went upstairs and explored the rest of her house. 3 bathrooms, 5 bedrooms, stacked with amazing technology. "Wow!" she walked around.

"It really is a nice place," said a familiar voice behind her.

*Jasmine whipped around and cried, "**Chriona Mrionte**." Chains shot out from the walls and wrapped around her father, pinning him. "I've been waiting for you to come back," she confessed with her sinister grin. "Practiced that just for you."*

"Well, here I am."

"You're a criminal?" she asked. "A...supervillain?"

"Yes, I believe so."

"How did you regenerate? How did you come back?"

"I did have some help..."

Jasmines ears perked up. "What?"

"Well we can't die! We are immortal. Just bring all of the pieces to the same room and, voila."

"Makes sense, I guess. Who helped you?"

"That does not matter. I just wanted to give you the offer one more time, daughter. Join me and together we shall seek revenge on the Zimmerman family and I shall make them pay and suffer for what they did to your mother and me. All you have to do is say the words."

He teleported out of the chains and reappeared behind her, causing them to clatter to the ground and then disappear.

"I can train you! I can be the father that wasn't there before. One more chance, Jasmine. Are you with me, or against me?" Jasmine raised her hands and the balcony doors behind him flew open. She pushed a blast outwards and her dad flew straight through the open doors and rolled onto the street and into a parked car down the road. Its alarm started to blare.

"Does that answer your question?" she yelled, lifting the car that he had slammed into. Just as she was going to hit him with it again, he teleported away.

MYLAN ALLEN

She then heard him inside her mind. You have just made a big mistake, Jasmine. You do not want me as an enemy. She threw some nasty words at him that made him go silent, and then she did the only rational thing that she could think of. Sleep.

CHAPTER IV: GODS

25.   TITAN

B y the time Arion had arrived at the theatre, the movie was done and Thalia was gone so he headed home for a good night's rest. It was the last month of school, so that put a smile on his face as he went to bed.

"Good Morning," Arion said to his dad once he got downstairs.

"'Morning," his dad replied.

"What's on the schedule for today?"

"I need to start training you. Your powers are only going to get more difficult to control."

Arion smiled. "Alright, after school?"

"Sure," his dad said.

"Sorry, got to run."

"Is that literal or are you taking the bus?"

Arion didn't answer but he did a small salute and said, "Later, dad," before dashing outside.

Arion arrived at school with minutes to spare. Those minutes ran by pretty quickly and before Arion even knew it, class was starting. Mr. Shuster, a balding, sour old man, (a.k.a, Arion's geography teacher) walked into the room after all of the students. "We have a new student joining us, although it is a bit…late in the year, I suppose, I'd like to introduce the class to Jasmine Roland."

Arion's mouth opened so wide he thought it might hit the floor. Jasmine walked into the room dressed up in a short denim skirt, red t-shirt and a denim vest with her blonde hair pulled back into a ponytail.

"Close your mouth," Jasmine whispered, barely audible enough for Arion to hear. "You'll catch flies."

Arion closed his mouth and simply stared, shaking his head. "Jasmine, my dear," Mr. Shuster said, quietly. "I'll have my two best students show you around the school. Thalia, Arion," he gestured towards them both, inviting them up.

"Go on now. Show her around," he motioned for them to leave.

Thalia extended her hand to Jasmine, beaming. "Hi I'm Thalia

Garcia."

"Nice to finally meet you," Jasmine said, giggling.

"Finally?" Thalia asked, confused.

"Oh, cr——" Arion began, before getting interrupted.

"——Yeah, Arion over here just won't shut up about you."

"Oh," Thalia stammered. "You two...know each other?"

"Unfortunately," Arion muttered.

"Yeah," Jasmine said, elbowing him in the ribs. Arion just walked down the hallway beside them saying nothing and adjusting his glasses.

"Well," Thalia said glancing at him, "if he says he's going to get some popcorn while you're on a date, do *not* expect him to come back."

"Oh so it was with Thalia?" Jasmine asked turning to him.

"Don't you da——" he started but Jasmine waved her hand and his mouth shut. She was using her telekinesis!

"I'm surprised you would ditch her for me, she's really pretty," Jasmine continued with a huge, devious smirk. "That was sweet though. Sorry," she then whispered to Thalia.

Thalia's face grew pale once she realized what Jasmine meant.

"You know what? I'm not feeling very well, I think I'm just going to go back to class," Thalia muttered turning away.

"No, Tal, it's not what you think," he turned back just in time to see her wipe tears from her face. "Thalia!"

"If it wasn't what I thought, you wouldn't have tried to stop her from telling me!" she nearly yelled.

"Thalia!" she raised her hand as if she was telling him to stop.

After she was out of sight Jasmine burst out laughing. "What the hell, Jaz?"

"I'm sorry," she laughed. "She was just so vulnerable and——" she looked at Arion in the eyes and probably realized that he was actually really angry.

"The one person, who's ever actually liked me and you blew it for me. Thanks a lot, *teammate!*"

"Arion, I didn't mean——"

"Save it!" he yelled, "and I actually thought that we could be friends! Show yourself around the damn school." As he walked away, he punched hole straight through a locker door and left her standing alone in the hallway.

26.   QUANTUM

Lucian woke up on the cold ground. He got up and anxiously looked around. He was in a circle surrounded by trees and three elderly people stood around him. He flipped open his palms and started forming energy balls. "You kidnapped the wrong guy—"

"Do not speak unless spoken to, my son," he then realized that it was the same three old people that had given him his abilities. He was in the same clearing that he was in when he received his powers.

"What are—" Lucian began.

"YOUR FATHER HAS CALLED FOR SILENCE!" boomed the woman. Lucian kept his mouth shut and listened.

"It is my understanding that you use your abilities publically and have joined a...superhuman hero team, yes?"

"Yes," he admitted wondering if that was such a bad thing.

"You go around the world fighting the forces of evil for the good of mankind?" asked the woman. "As a *guardian?*"

"Yes."

"You are accomplishing the exact mission that your father had planned out for you."

His father began to speak, "I only met with your mother for the sole purpose of creating offspring. We thought that we would need successors as we are becoming older, it's been *thousands* of years."

"Successors?" he asked. He chose to *ignore* the comment about his mother.

"We placed limited control of all three of the entities inside of you so that when you found a person worthy enough, you could *share* your power with them and if they shall perish, you would regain their abilities until you have found another person and it continues on and on forever in an *endless* cycle. You would keep whichever one suited you the best and whichever one you had the most control over. The master of a new generation, continuing our legacy."

Lucian looked at each and every one of them. "Why do I have these powers? Who am *I?*" Lucian asked.

The woman sighed. "We are gods. All *four* of us, are higher beings compared to mortals."

"I stopped believing in God a *very* long time ago," Lucian said standing firmly.

"Ah, yes. You're referring to The *Christian* God, yes? He exists too. One of the more powerful gods."

The black man chuckled. "*All* of the Gods exist, Lucian. This is all *much* bigger than you think, you are still thinking like a mortal, not like a god. We were never documented by the mortals like the rest, because we transfer our abilities too often to our offspring or someone who is worthy, every few thousand years or so. Greek, Roman, Hindu, Norse, Egyptian, Christian and countless other Gods exist. You only know the half of it, Lucian."

"How did I get here?"

"We created a portal through your own power to bring you here," the woman admitted.

"Where is *here?*"

"You are in Aethera, also known as neutral earth, limbo, even. The center of the three realms of the gods. Aesur is above, also known as heaven or Elysium and then there is Aedalis, hell or the underworld.

"The gods work together," his dad began. "*Zeus* works with *Jupiter* and *Thor* for lightning, sky and thunder. *Poseidon, Neptune* and other water deities work together and so on."

"This is where you can come for guidance from *any* god, past or present and as you have realized, we can communicate with you telepathically."

"You can watch earth passing by every single day as you train."

"Can I tell my friends that I'm okay?"

"Of course, *immediately* after your five earth years of training."

27.   CIRCE

Jasmine had read the minds of the students around her to discover her surroundings and then went back to the class, taking her awkward seat in between Thalia and Arion. She had realized that she had taken it too far with Thalia. She told herself that it was just a joke but, the truth was, Jasmine wanted her to feel bad. She was jealous and hated Thalia for no valid reason, except that she liked Arion.

"Thalia," Jasmine said after 10 minutes of listening to Mr. Shuster speak. Thalia turned and her eyes were red. "I didn't mean to do anything back there. I'm sorry, it wasn't like that we were just—" Thalia cut her off.

"You're sorry!?" she hissed in a whisper. "It's not you that should be sorry! It's him!" She gestured towards Arion with her head.

"But that's what I'm trying to—"

"Ms. Roland," Mr. Shuster interrupted. "I'm glad that you have made yourself comfortable in my class but would you mind sharing whatever you're talking about with the rest of us?" The bell rang and the class left in a hurry before Jasmine had to say anything.

"Can I show you to your next class?" Thalia asked.

"We have a five minute break in between classes."

"Sure," Jasmine said pushing all of the guilt that she could out of the word. They walked to their class around the long way but Jasmine couldn't help sneaking a look back and watch Arion turn the other corner and she sighed.

"So, Jaz," Thalia started. "Can I call you Jaz? Where are you from? What do your parents do? Tell me about yourself."

"Umm, sure. My parents are from...Queens, New York but they moved here. Closer to business stuff."

Thalia obviously brushed off Jaz's simple answer and continued. "Well, I'm born here but my mom was born in The Dominican Republic and...I didn't know my dad. My last name is Garcia and I like to play tennis, dance and just hang around."

"I like flying." Jasmine winced and knew that she had blown it.

"Oh, like...vacationing?"

"Yeah, sure, something like that." Lucky for Jasmine she had arrived at her next class, math and didn't have to cover her slip-up too much. Arion walked in after her but

Thalia went on to a different class.

Jasmine introduced herself to Ms. Clark, a young, blonde, twenty-something-year-old woman, and took a seat at the back of the class, away from Arion. Jasmine felt good and bad at the same time. She wanted to be happy with Arion and she wanted him to be happy with her but he didn't seem to know whether he wanted to be with Thalia or her.

She decided to read his mind. What the hell is that? Jasmine, is that you?

Arion looked back at her and she nodded. I sensed you intruding. It was like a ringing in my ears.

Of course, Jasmine thought to herself, perfect.

What's perfect? Arion asked.

Wait...you can hear me?

I guess. Do you think it's me?

No, I think...I think I'm getting stronger.

"*Jaz, your nose,*" *he called out loud while Ms. Clark was talking.*

Jasmine touched under her nose and felt blood on her fingers. She jumped up, hand cupped over her face and ran to the bathroom.

28. <u>TITAN</u>

Arion knew quite a bit about psychic powers, or at least enough to know that if you overexert yourself with them, you get headaches and a bloody nose.

Arion watched her leave and then turned his attention to the front, listening to Ms. Clark drone on and on until the bell finally rang. It was lunch so after Arion ate he went to talk to Thalia. "Tal," he started.

"I mean, I know that we weren't like dating or anything, but the one time that we actually *have* a date, you ditch me for another girl. Not cool, Arion."

"It's not like that!"

"Then why did you ditch me for her?"

"I..." he stopped himself. He couldn't tell her without revealing his secret. And he couldn't reveal his secret without revealing Jasmines. "Never mind." Thalia walked away, disgusted, muttering something in Spanish.

"Even when she's mad at me, she still sounds hot," Arion whispered to himself, shaking his head. Jasmine walked into the lunchroom looking better than before and all cleaned up. "Jaz," Arion called out, waving her over.

"Are we...okay?"

"Almost, I need to ask a favour..."

"Yeah, sure."

"I need to tell Thalia my secret...and to do that I'd need to reveal yours too, but I won't if you don't want me to."

"Um, yeah, I guess that's okay."

"Whoa, seriously?" Arion asked, surprised. He had expected a flat-out *No,* but he had asked anyways.

"Only if you really trust her. Do you?"

"More than anything and I've known her since we were in the first grade."

"And it'll make everything good between us?" Jasmine asked eagerly.

"Yeah," he promised. "Definitely."

"Good, do what you will, I didn't really want a secret identity anyways. I'm debating..."

"Thank you so much, Jaz!" He picked her up and spun her around in a hug.

"Ouch! Chill, just because I'm immortal and will heal, doesn't mean I don't feel pain."

"Sorry!" he turned just in time to see Thalia walking out the front door.

He found her talking to her friends by the wall of the school.

"I'm not normal, okay?" he told her after they had gone somewhere private.

"Oh, trust me, I know that," she turned, ready to walk away.

"No, I mean...you heard about those superheroes, on TV, right? *Titan, Circe, Quantum, Atlantica* and *Hyperion?*"

"Yeah, of course. But...their names weren't even released publically yet, were they?"

"Well... no. I know this because...I'm Titan and Jasmine is Circe. That's where we were last night, together. Saving Italy from hundreds of rampaging wildcats."

"I don't have time for this crap!" She began to walk away.

"Wait," Arion said. "I'll prove it."

She slowly turned around, indicating that he had gotten her attention and he appeared behind her using his super speed.

"Um..." was all she could get out as she spun around. He took her hips and ever-so-carefully lifted her up at least three feet off of the ground, before putting her back down.

"Give me a place, any place. Where have you always wanted to go?"

"Miami," she admitted, "never been." He picked her up in his arms and she wrapped her arms around his neck, head nuzzled in his shoulder and he ran all the way down to Miami.

He put her down in the sand of the beach. She looked out over the water and then quickly turned, threw her arms around his neck and kissed him, all of his worries washing away.

29. QUANTUM

"5 YEARS!?" Lucian nearly yelled, his eyes glowing red. His father was showing him around Aethera, the connection between all the worlds.

"I understand that it may seem like a long time to you now, but you will live on for thousands, maybe even *millions* of years, much longer than any of those humans that you have befriended."

Lucian didn't bother telling him that Arion should stop aging at around 30, Jasmine was immortal and Hyperion could probably live forever too, being an entity of light.

"All of that might be true," his dad answered, probably reading his mind, "but if death shall reach them prior to that, then what? You live watching everyone else die. That is why I am not still on earth. I live here with the near immortal or immortal gods."

"I don't want to live here!"

"Lucian, son," he started.

"You're not my father!" As soon as he said it his dad shifted, growing younger until he looked like an exact replica of his dad from his fuzzy memory. "Better?" Lucian said nothing.

"Hey!?" Someone called out. Lucian and his dad both

turned towards the sound.

"Zeus!" His dad called to the man. The man had a scruffy white beard, tan-coloured skin and was wearing casual clothes. He looked more like he was going to the store rather than being the almighty and all powerful ruler of the Greek Gods.

"Who's this?" he asked reaching out for Lucian's hand.

"I'm Lucian, his...son," he winced on the word. "Also known as Quantum, Master of Manipulation."

"Lucian," he nodded his head and then turned to Lucian's father. "Do you mind if I speak with your father, alone? Please."

"Sure." They walked out of earshot and began to have a conversation. Lucian only caught a few words,

"Ares...earth..." and, "disappeared."

Lucian just stood there, waiting. His father walked back to him after a few minutes. "I will call you back here whenever I please. If you do not come back here when I call you, there *will* be consequences, Lucian. Am I understood?"

"Yes," Lucian whispered, staring at the floor.

"There is some trouble that I must attend to." His dad used both hands to push him backwards through another rainbow-coated portal. A large red beam swirled past his father and slammed into his chest as he flew through the portal. The next thing he knew, he was skipping across the water in the exact same place where he was abducted.

30.   CIRCE

Jasmine was still at the school, alone, because the only two friends that she had made were probably halfway around the world or kissing on the moon. She sighed and waited in the library until the bell rang. Right after the bell rang, Arion zoomed in carrying Thalia. Jasmine—luckily—was the only person to see it.

Jasmine walked up to him and punched him in the arm. "What!?" he asked.

"Stop doing that! Be more silent and stealthy with your speed or you'll compromise both *of our identities."*

Arion excused himself from Thalia, sealing it with a kiss

and she walked back to class with Jasmine and Arion falling behind. "Thank you, Jaz, this really means a lot to me and guess what! I heard the school bell ring from all the way in Miami, I just focused on it and, heard it when it went off. I'm getting the hang of this whole superpower thing."

"Uh-huh. That's great. I got a call from Corbin while you were gone."

"That reminds me..." he said. He tapped his communicator, turning it back on. "What'd he say?"

"Lucian is back."

"Back?"

"Yesterday, he disappeared after the fight with the wildcats. Speaking of which, Corbin has no lead on that. He wants us to be there right after school, okay?"

"Yeah, sure."

By the time they finished their little conversation, they were back at the same class as the period before lunch. Jasmine sighed, "Ms. Clark, again?"

"She teaches us English. Don't get used to it, you only have a few weeks left."

"True, very true. Talk to you later?"

"Sure."

The class passed by quickly and the next thing she knew, it was gym class. The girls went into their change room, as did the guys.

Jasmine pulled Thalia over. "Want me to show you something cool?" she asked.

"Cooler than you and my boyfriend being the world's newest superheroes?" she asked in a whisper, "unlikely."

*"Ha." Jasmine looked around making sure no one was watching and waved her hand. "**Phantumus Exponesis**," she chanted. It was one of the few spells that she had been working on and now fully perfected.*

"What did you do?" Thalia asked looking in the mirror and seeing nothing.

"We're invisible. Phantoms. We can walk through walls, disappear and fly."

"Very...unique."

"Yeah, just keep holding on to me."

"Where are we going?"

"The boys change room of course."

"You're really starting to grow on me, Jasmine."

"Oh, you just wait," Jasmine said with her signature smirk, *"you just wait."*

31. <u>TITAN</u>

Arion tugged off his shirt and threw it into his gym locker. From behind him, *Jack Foley* walked up and slapped him in the back of the head. Arion heard a heavy crack and his vision blurred for a split second. But, he also saw Foley grab his hand and grimace in pain.

"Thick-skulled freak!" he said and all his friends laughed and hi-fived him—on his other hand.

"What a cliché!" Carter Wilkinson exclaimed after they had left. He was Ollie's son and one of Arion's best friends. "He's been bullying us since we met him in the first grade, captain of the football team, dating the hottest—" Arion coughed, "err—arguably the hottest girl in school—also the head cheerleader, Samantha Michaels—and to top it off he has the gang who always laughs at everything he says! Did I miss anything?"

"Not at all," Arion agreed.

"Hurry up, if not, coach is going to kill you with laps," he said jogging out.

Arion suddenly heard something. The flow of some sort of liquid and the fluttering of eyelashes, as if someone was blushing. He twirled around. "Hello?" no answer. "I know someone's here!" he yelled out.

The spots cleared from his vision and he looked around. His vision flared and he saw one purple-coloured skeleton and one white skeleton with blue auras where skin covers the bones. Their bones were glowing and they were just standing there watching him. Arion tripped backwards over his own feet and landed on his butt and started crab-walking backwards.

One of them whispered, "He can see us?"

"Apparently. Seems like he can hear us too."

"Jasmine? Thalia?" he asked. They both faded into view.

"How did you see us?" Jasmine asked putting on her pouty face, which Arion found so hot. He realized that he was staring. Thalia scowled at him while Jasmine giggled to herself. He felt a familiar ringing in his ears.

"You didn't!" he yelled at her.

"Didn't what?" Jasmine asked, biting her lip, trying not to smile.

"Read my mind!?"

"Anyway!" Thalia rudely interrupted. "How'd you see us?"

"I kind of...x-rayed the place."

"What?" they both screamed out immediately covering themselves with their arms.

"I saw your skeletons, not through your clothes," he said. "Guess I'm not that good yet." They both sighed. "Don't worry, ladies, I'll get better!" He winked and dashed out of the room before either of them could protest.

32. QUANTUM

Lucian was walking, in civilian clothes, behind Corbin and a few agents. Within a few minutes he was sitting inside an interrogation room. It was pure white, every single wall, but the table and the three chairs, were black.

"Don't be fooled by the room, Lucian," Corbin said walking in and taking a seat in a chair on the other side of the table. "We're not interrogating you...per se."

"Whatever," Lucian said. "You know that I can get out

of here whenever I want, right?" Corbin looked Lucian in the eyes and he was hesitant.

"Actually, you can't. We call this: *Detainment*. Charmed by the greatest spell casters and reinforced with the most alien metals, you aren't going anywhere, son."

"Are you trying to convince *me?* Or *yourself?*"

Corbin ignored the question. "Where'd you disappear to?"

"That is classified information. I'm under order not to tell you," Lucian said, grinning.

"Lucian, we are not *asking* you, if you do not answer our question then we will be forced to detain and arrest you for obstruction of justice."

Lucian rolled his eyes and stood up. "I was with my dad."

"Your father died years ago, Lucian! Stop treating this like a game!"

"Ha, that's not what the gods think," Lucian muttered.

Lucian raised his hands and the wall bent under his telekinetic grip and he hovered through the hole. "So much power for such a small being," he muttered to himself.

After a few minutes of walking down the hallway he heard a voice boom, "HALT!" behind him. He turned slowly, hands in his pockets and saw dozens of armed men in the wide hallway. "Alright, kid. No one wants to hurt you so how about you just come with us."

"How about I just leave?"

"Corbin said to detain you at all costs," the man replied. "Safeties off!" The man raised his gun and the clicks of their guns cocking ran throughout the hallway. Lucian threw back his head and laughed.

The soldier looked in his hand and saw a big water gun. "OPEN FIRE!" he yelled. Lucian *literally* didn't lift a finger and caused all of the bullets to crush against a force field of his own creation, barely an inch from his body. He continued to walk with dozens of bullets ricocheting everywhere.

"I don't have time for this!" he said. He flew upwards

and phased straight through the ceiling. When he landed on the floor of the other level he examined his hands.

"I'm glad I awaited a younger god. So much...*power,*" he said to himself. Then the alarm went off and the screeching noises and flashing red lights poured into the corridor.

IT'S NOT ME! He tried to scream but the words couldn't—wouldn't—escape his mouth. If felt as though he was a spectator inside his own body. He could see and hear but everything else was gone. He had no control.

They can't hear you, Son of Energy. You are dealing with Ares, God of War, said a deep voice inside him. Then came the laugh inside of him, the most evil thing that Lucian had *ever* heard.

33. CIRCE

Jasmine and Thalia left after Arion told them about his new power and went to their gym class. Jaz had to go through the introductions for the third or fourth time that day. Thankfully, Thalia and Jasmine were almost the same size so she borrowed some gym clothes from her.

They were playing soccer while the guys did track and field as a fun, last-month-of-school activity. *Jasmine, she heard in her head and jumped.*

What!? This is a complete invasion of privacy, you know!

I need your help, he said. You're the only one who can see me and tell me how fast I'm going, tell me to ease up or speed up a bit.

But I actually like soccer, she complained.

Jaz, I need to keep my identity a secret until I gain full control over my abilities, just help me out, he begged.

Fine, she thought, finally giving in.

Thanks I owe you one.

Actually, I think you owe me two or three—

"JAZ!" Thalia yelled.

"Yeah!?"

"We've been calling you for the past five minutes, you're on my team."

"Kids," Corbin said through her communicator. "We

need you all here, now."

"Where and why?" she whispered, discreetly.

"At Area 52, it's Lucian."

"Actually guys, I'm not feeling very well, I think I'll just go inside," she announced to her class.

"Okay," Thalia said, as if she knew why she was leaving.

Arion, you coming?

I'm already dressed.

Within a few minutes Jasmine was soaring just above Arion—sticking to land, as usual—on their way to Area 52.

"Oh my God." Jasmine said. There was smoke rising from the building and explosions were going off, spraying sand and dust everywhere. "Lucian is doing this?"

"Don't know," Meredith said, leaping off of a cloud. She was wearing an ocean-blue bikini bottom and an ocean-blue bandeau top, only covering her chest and a small domino mask, barely hiding her identity. "I just got here."

Hyperion teleported into view next to them. "What took you so long?" Arion asked.

"I estimated how long it would take you guys to get

here."

"What's the problem?" Arion demanded.

Jasmine raised her index and middle finger to her head and concentrated.

"Lucian is definitely the problem."

"What?" Meredith squeaked.

"Let's go, doll," Hyperion said reaching for her hand.

There was a gust of wind and the entire team fell and tumbled backwards. "There's no need for that, Blake." Lucian floated out of the hole in the side of the building. Then he scoffed at the sight of them. " This is who they sent to oppose a god?"

"You aren't a god!" Arion called to him.

"Lucian is just a minor god for now," he chuckled, talking about himself. He had the same voice but behind that, there was something more. Something darker. "The only way that I could possess him is if he could take it. If Lucian was a human or a superhuman he would've been burned to a crisp."

"Who are you?" Meredith asked shakily. "And what have you done with Lucian?"

"I am Ares, God of War. Just ask your telepath," he nodded at Jasmine, *"she can find Lucian somewhere up here,"* he tapped his—or Lucian's—head.

Help me, she heard in his head, just barely, but she heard it.

"He's there," she said. *"Deep, under thousands of other things. Disgusting, evil, 10 years of therapy kinds of things."*

"Well let's get him out, Guardians!" Arion called charging.

34. <u>TITAN</u>

Hyperion flashed up to where Ares was floating and brought two giant fists made out of pure light down on top of him, swatting him to the ground where Arion was waiting, he delivered an uppercut which sent him straight back towards Hyperion and he knocked her towards Meredith who enveloped him in barrage of water and sand.

"It's difficult fighting a teammate, isn't it?" Ares-in-Lucian's-body asked. "You make your team as powerful as possible but if some ever turned you'd have no way to stop them. If Titan here turned, who would fight him? Lucian? Jasmine? Who's powerful enough? The amount of gods that I have faced is well into the thousands and I have won every single battle. Do you know why!?" he demanded. "Strategy!" He zoomed up into the air so fast Arion's ears popped from the sonic boom.

"Where's he headed?" Arion yelled, watching him fly away. "Follow him!"

He heard coughing behind him. Corbin stumbled through the dust and said, "He's heading to *Area 25: Supervillain District*, 188 kilometers south of here. He's breaking them out!"

"Dammit! Guys!" he yelled into his communicator, "He's breaking out the villains."

"Which ones?" Meredith demanded.

"All of them!" he yelled. "It'll be a full blown war!"

"You'll all be defenseless. Some villains have been in there for decades with hate for yours and Jasmines parents specifically. Be careful!"

"Jasmines parents?" Arion asked, confused.

"Never mind," yelled Corbin. "GO!"

"Thanks." He sprinted to Area 25 in three seconds.

Ares was standing near the wall of a huge stone building, guns and snipers trained on him and The Guardians.

"You don't have the power to get in." Arion said. Ares backed up until he was brushing against the wall.

"Don't I?" he asked. He began to sink into the wall, phasing directly through it.

"That's new," Arion muttered.

"Where is he?" a soldier asked. Arion concentrated on finding him. He closed his eyes and when they reopened, the wall in-between himself and Lucian——Ares——was gone. He saw him running in the hallway. "He's going straight and... now he's making a left at the main corridor. Looks like he's heading for..."

"The control panel!" A guard yelled. "How do you know?"

"I have my fathers' eyes." He ran as fast as he could through the corridor and ended up in front of Ares. "I can't let you pass me, Lucian."

"MY NAME IS ARES!" He shot a purple blast of energy at Arion but he easily dodged it coming up to Ares with a right hook. Ares soared backwards into the wall and bounced from one side to the other. He wiped his bleeding lip with his sleeve. "Is that all that you've got, mortal?" he spat the word as if it was an insult.

Arion ran at him but Ares grabbed his arm, using his own momentum to throw him into a wall. After he hit the wall, Arion had a metallic taste in his mouth. The taste of blood.

"Ares uses magic," he muttered. "Good to know." Ares ran into the control room but Arion got up and quickly threw a left hook. Ares let it phase through his head and then lifted his foot to kick Arion straight in the chest and out of the door.

"You mortals——" he paused to punch Arion, "——all think you are at the top of the food chain! But you aren't!" he yelled wrapping his hands around Arion's neck. "You are nothing to the immortal, God of War!" Ares lifted him by his throat and punched him hard enough to dent the steel walls from meters away just by pure force. It was the perfect timing because all of the guards ran out right into his path causing Arion to smash into all of them.

"Stop this!" Arion heard Lucian say through his own mouth.

"Never! War is power! War is everywhere! All that it needs is a little, push!" Ares flipped the switches around until finally the open sequence override popped up. "I need more power! More...war! I. Win!" He pushed the button and dozens of alarms went off as each and every cell door in the building was opened. Arion ran and raised his fist. Ares exited Lucian's body and floated up into the air but Arion was already moving too fast. His fist flew into Lucian's face and he dropped like a sack of potatoes.

35.   QUANTUM

"Are you sure that he's gone?" Corbin asked slamming his hands on the table.

"YES!" Lucian yelled. He was in the same interrogation room from earlier that day when he was Ares, with Arion, Jasmine and Corbin. The only difference was the giant hole in the wall. He was holding an ice-pack to his head from Arion's wonderful hit.

"I can't sense anything other than Lucian," Jasmine said.

"You're sure?"

"Nope, just said it to get your hopes up. *Of course*, I'm sure!"

Corbin sighed. "Can you tell us where you were and why you were possessed by some freak named Ares?"

"He wasn't just some *freak.*" They all turned and looked at him, listening intently.

"He was the actual Greek God of war and bloodshed." Lucian explained everything to them that he knew about Aethera, Aesur and Aedalis. "I guess Ares somehow possessed me before I left. I know it was him—the real deal—because I could feel his power surging through me."

"We can't fight gods," Arion said, "we can *barely* fight supervillains and one of our teammates was just *injured* in the battle against them."

"Well this *God* just let out every single supervillain that we have caught on the planet over the past 30 years! 93 villains. Abilities ranging from breathing underwater to controlling gravity itself. You can all leave. Now. I've got an *unimaginable* amount of paperwork to do! You guys better get started on finding those villains. *Now!*"

All three of them were walking away from Area 52. "Those villains couldn't have gotten far, right?" Arion asked to break the silence.

"Not necessarily, they were all helping each other, someone with flight and super strength could carry bunches of people. Or earth manipulators could've lifted a slab of hardened sand or pavement with dozens of people on them."

"That would explain all of the holes in the ground," Arion muttered.

"I'm sorry, guys," Lucian said.

"For?" They both asked at the same time.

"For everything, for causing this mess. I...I think I'm quitting the team. I'm going to go do the training with my...dad."

"Lucian—" Jasmine began to say but, he held up his hand before taking off into the sky.

CHAPTER V: TRAINING

36.   CIRCE

*J*asmine watched Lucian fly off. "He can't just quit, can he!?" she exclaimed once he was out of earshot.

"He has his own free-will, he can quit if he wants. Next time I see him, I'll try and convince him not to though. Want me to walk you home?"

"Well it isn't really walking, now is it?" she said smiling at the fact that he *wanted* to walk her home in the first place.

They arrived at Jasmines house within a few minutes. "Nice place," he said.

"Thanks." They stood there awkwardly for a few seconds.

"Well, my dad said he's going to train me so, I have to go but, call me if you need me?"

"For sure." He zoomed out of there and probably back to his house.

Just before she reached the stairs there was a knock at the door. She went back to open it and there stood Arion again. "My dad knows a lot about psychic powers and magic and stuff so... I was wondering if you wanted to come and train, make your powers stronger and...stuff." He smiled and it seemed as if his teeth sparkled. She heard herself say something and the next thing she knew, he was carrying her in a run to his house.

"Why are you so late?" his dad asked.

"Lucian was possessed by a god, sorry." His dad nodded. Jasmine still didn't understand how Arion could be so...cool with absolutely everything. Like, Gods exist? Boring.

"We dealt with a few of them back in my day too. No one believed us of course." His eyes shifted to Jasmine and he raised an eyebrow at Arion.

"Dad, I was wondering if you could...you know, train her too. I know that you could help her get stronger." Thinking about getting stronger made her think about her own dad's offer to train her, but she quickly shook the thought out of her head.

"Well...I guess it couldn't hurt," he mumbled.

"Yeah. Thanks," Jasmine replied. *As soon as he was out of earshot she said, "He doesn't like me much, does he?"*

Arion shrugged. "I have no clue."

37. TITAN

"It's good having a main magic manipulator on your team because if you ever get out of line, she can hurt you," his dad began. "Your mom and I...well, we got our abilities from radiation, right?"

"That's what I'm told," Arion said with a smile.

"Well, radiation comes in many different ways, shapes, forms and spectrums. The biggest source of radiation currently is the sun. Different suns and different forms of radiation gave us different powers.

"My people, Zonarians, had powers on my home planet because we were very close to the sun. Your mother's planet was agreeably further from the sun and while they still had powers, they decided to use the radioactive core of their planet to gain energy. They harvested too much and...well, let's just say there aren't too many Lyriics left in the universe. I just want you to be careful with your energies. Make sure that you know what you're doing."

"Now, mental training." He smiled and led them to the practice room. "If you guys are on a team together, you have to work together. If you can't get the upper hand on a villain, switch with a teammate or put it off until someone else can. Jasmine, try...expanding your telekinetic field. Just concentrate on a...shield. Cover your entire body with repulsing energy."

"Why?"

"How do you think any other telekinetic becomes invulnerable? Or flies?" Jasmine raised her hands and concentrated on her field getting bigger and surrounding her but she couldn't.

"It's not working," she sighed, lowering her hands.

"Are you trying?" Arion asked.

"Of course, I'm trying!"

"Try harder, Jasmine," Arthur said before he shot her.

38.   <u>Q</u>UANTUM

Lucian flew up high, higher than he'd ever gone before, besides the time when he flew across space. He adjusted his communicator so that his message would be sent solely to Meredith.

"Hey, Meredith, can we...talk?" he asked.

"Yeah, sure," she replied after a few seconds. "Meet up?"

"Your place?"

"Sure," Lucian flew a bit easier because it seemed as though Meredith was fine and they were still friends. He couldn't have been sure after he disappeared, came back possessed by a sadistic god and because of the breakout, broke her arm.

Cruising, Lucian was there in about 20 minutes. He arrived at her island and floated down to the front door. She opened the door, her right arm in a sling. "Hey," she said. "What's up?"

"Nothing. Can I um..." he gestured inside.

"Yeah, sure, come in."

"Thanks. I'm quitting the team."

"What!?" she exclaimed. "Why?"

"It's becoming too much, I might just go do my five-year training."

"FIVE YEAR TRAINING!?" she demanded.

"Oh yeah," Lucian muttered, remembering that he didn't tell Meredith the story.

He explained everything that had happened with his dad while Meredith listened intently. She reached for his hand and he didn't protest.

"Please, stay," she whispered. He looked into her eyes and saw them rippling blue. He knew that he'd *never* be able to say no to her.

"I'll think about it," he said with a smile. "Did you know that some hydrokinetics were skilled enough to heal them-selves with water?"

"Your comic book nerd is showing!" she joked. "But, no, I didn't, and I'm sure as hell going to try." She walked to her in-ground pool and Lucian followed. She sat down at the edge of the pool and slowly slid off into the water.

"See, water is the connective tissue between everything. All living things are made out of it, we need it to survive, and it takes up more than 70% of the planet. Just concentrate on letting the water *inside* you. Let it soothe you and surround you. *Become* the water."

She went underwater and stayed down there for a good 5 minutes. Lucian just waited and waited until she finally popped up, arm out of the sling, healed perfectly. She climbed out of the water and did a running jump and Lucian caught her, she wrapped both arms around him and kissed him.

"Thanks," she said.

"For what?"

"For helping me discover a new ability."

"That was nothing."

"And for this," she kissed him again.

He laughed. "Now *that* was *definitely* something."

"I've never really been *hurt* before...I don't really socialize or anything like that, much."

"Yeah, I've noticed. Why do you stay so...*isolated?* Why don't you come back to the world?"

"I don't really...like interacting with other people."

"So you get this huge island, just for you? Because the government found out you had superpowers?" She nodded. "Why don't you get some more people? To live here?"

"Nobody else is like me." She sat down with her feet in the pool and smiled. "I'm one of a kind."

Lucian sucked the excess atoms of his clothes leaving him in swimming shorts and he sat down next to her. "You are *definitely* one of a kind." Lucian jumped into the pool and pulled her under the water with him, until they heard the muffled sound of an explosion.

39.   CIRCE

After the bullet was fired Jasmine screamed but it bounced right off of her. "What the hell, dad?" Arion yelled.

"What!? She's alive, isn't she?"

"Yeah, but what if she didn't get the shield up!?"

"Son, she's immortal, it wouldn't have done anything anyways!"

"Oh, yeah—" he stopped mid-sentence and tilted his head a little bit, listening. Jasmine looked at Arion's dad but he simply put a finger to his lips and tapped his ears. She nodded, a silent understanding.

"There are explosions, and fire."

"Pinpoint it, son."

"Meredith's island. Lucian is there too."

"You, go. I need to talk to Jasmine. Don't listen in."

"Fine!" he said with a sigh. He pushed the button on his belt and sped off as his suit expanded around his body.

"Yes, Mr. Zimmerman."

"I understand many things, just because I don't have powers, doesn't mean my other skills go away."

"Okay then."

"I know that you like Arion as more than a friend and I won't tell him that." She felt her face heat up and turn red. "There's no need for embarrassment, there's a twinkle in your eyes whenever you look at him, but also regret. Pretty obvious if you ask me."

Jasmine forced a smile. "Okay, so what if I do?"

"I also know that he's with Thalia. I need you to prom-ise me something though. Lyriics are very honest, noble and sacrificial people naturally. He will do anything to protect those that he loves and believe it or not he likes the both of you. Promise me that no matter what happens, you'll never stop protecting him. Whether it's from the sidelines or in a fight, have his back because he'll always have yours."

"I-I promise."

"Thank you, Jasmine. I know what your dad did to his mom and there is absolutely no way that I could blame you. I might seem...distant towards you but I don't mean to be. You just...look so much like your father.

"I met you when you were just a baby, you know. I was actually the one that dropped you off at the foster home after your parents...were gone. I don't want the sins of your par-ents and all of the other heroes before you guys to affect your relationship. Don't tell him about your parents just yet. Wait until its right. Now, go save your friends."

Jasmine nodded and then took off, soaring through the air to the center of the Atlantic. She saw the fire raging from the sky once she got there.

"No!" She flew in as fast as she could, straight down to-ward the island. She immediately telekinetically picked up the water from the ocean and threw it onto the fire. Arion circled the fires over and over again trying to cut off the oxygen so that the fire couldn't spread but they all just stopped as if one giant gust of wind had hit them.

All of the fires died down except for one. It was one of the twins that Lucian had caught before, Nexus. She was standing in front of Jasmine, hands behind her back. Arion, Hyperion and Lucian stood by Jasmine's sides

Everyone was there except for Meredith. "The whole team, here for me?" she asked in a mocking voice. "You shouldn't have."

Jaz, she heard in her mind. Arion's voice, Meredith is here, I don't know where, just....somewhere. Keep a lookout!

"I suppose you guys are looking for this?" she moved her hand which then pulled a cage of fire, from a hole in the ground with Meredith in the center, unconscious. "All you have to do is hack into the government files and you have a

list of weaknesses and most recent addresses. Meredith Rain-waters, right?" she asked, sarcastically.

Lucian let out a battle cry and flew straight at Nexus. There was a crash in the sand and Lucian was stopped by a huge, rocky fist flying straight into his face. He tumbled backwards and completely destroyed some of Meredith's jungle. "Long time, no see," Rage said to Arion.

"You're working with Nexus now?" Lucian demanded.

"More like teaming up against a common threat." Arion took a step forward but Rage wagged his finger at him. "Ah, ah, ah," he clucked. Huntress, Arc and Pixie dropped down from the sky. "Five against four. You up for these odds?"

"Always," Arion replied before running at Rage and tackling him, taking them skipping like rocks along the water.

40.   TITAN

Arion threw punch after punch but Rage blocked and countered, eventually lifting his knee into Arion's stomach and flipping him up into the air. Rage flew up to meet him and gave him a right hook sending him back towards the island.

Rage flew after him at speeds that seemed too high for anyone that size. His giant wings pushed so hard that Arion could hear the air being split with every flap. It was taking everything inside him not to scream out in fear of soaring through the air. He landed on his feet but tumbled backwards through the sand. Rage landed in a fury of sand in front of him and wailed on him. After every single punch Rage seemed to be getting stronger.

"Rage!" Huntress yelled. "That's enough!" Rage continued hitting Arion. "STOP!" she yelled again. He got up and began walking back to his friends.

"Why are you guys doing this?" Arion demanded. "What could possibly be in it for you!?"

"We get our lives back!" Rage turned around and kicked him right in the stomach sending him flying through the trees.

"Put it under," Huntress said, nodding at the island. Arion watched helplessly as Rage strapped a collar onto Meredith's neck and threw her into the ocean. "What did you do?" Lucian screamed at them. "WHAT DID YOU DO TO HER!?" he tried to fly at them but Arc sent a wave of electricity at him, forcing him back to the ground.

"You'll see!" Rage growled. "We're *The Superiors*. And The Guardians are in our way! If you stay in our way, we will destroy each and every last one of you!" He grabbed Arc, and flew up. Pixie, Huntress and Nexus—through shooting flames at the ground—flew after him. Lucian jumped into the ocean and resurfaced a few seconds later with an unconscious Meredith. Her skin was glowing blue and the water began to swirl around her. Her eyes emitted a radiant, blue light and her hair changed to a glowing turquoise colour. A huge number of waves crashed into the island, leaving them barely hanging on with their lives.

Hyperion stood by Lucian and Meredith—whom had been protected by Lucian's force field—and spoke to him but Arion couldn't focus on what he was saying over the crashing waves.

Hyperion realized that they were getting nowhere and came to meet Arion. "Do you think you could get everyone out of here?"

"I think so. I feel better now. Healing factor, I guess."

"Take them all away from here. Jasmine is unconscious and you'll have to be careful through the waves, those are tsunami sized, they'll probably be dead or worse within minutes."

"Good luck, bro." They gripped each other's hands in a firm handshake. "See what you can do."

Arion zoomed off and picked up Jasmine first. He put her on the beach and left right after for Lucian. Once he got there, Lucian was still next to Meredith. "We've got to go man!" he yelled over the crashing of the waves.

"I won't leave her!"

"Trust me, Lucian. Get out of here! We got this." Lucian hesitated for a second but sighed and flew up into the air. He hovered for a second, looking at Meredith before blasting off to shore.

"The collar is made out of pure electricity, compliments of Arc, I'm assuming. If we touch it, it hurts her and us."

"How are we going to do this?"

"I don't know, man. It's amplifying her powers by the hundreds. It doesn't even look like she knows what she's doing!" he yelled over the roar of the waves.

"Take her under the water," Arion exclaimed.

"What?" Hyperion asked, confused.

"If we take her deep enough, it might short the collar, right?"

Arion demanded.

"I don't know——" Hyperion began.

"It's our best chance!" he interrupted.

Arion watched as Hyperion, lifted Meredith and then pulled her under the water. They'd only been underwater for a few seconds before the explosion came. A chute of water shot up, covering the entire island, pulling it under the water. Arion jumped into the air and when the water rushed under him, he assumed a diving position and dove right in.

He concentrated on seeing through the water and it worked, his X-ray vision turned on. He saw two skeletons floating under the water and he kicked his feet as hard as he could and grabbed them both. He finally brought them back to shore, just before they were crushed by the sinking island. He laid them beside Jasmine. Arion saw Lucian give him a nod.

"You did great," Lucian told him, before Arion blacked out too.

41.   QUANTUM

Lucian dealt with all of the cameras flashing in his face

and pushed the people away from him and his team. So many questions were being fired at once, he couldn't even concentrate. But then he heard someone say, "Close your eyes," he did as he was told and he saw the flash of yellow light through his eyelids.

The next thing he knew there was a glowing yellow platform beneath his feet and he was being lifted into the air along with his 3 other unconscious teammates and Hyperion, whom was controlling the platform.

"Thanks for the save, Blake," he told Hyperion once they were near Area 52.

"Call me that again and I'll *permanently* blind you."

Lucian gulped. "Oh yeah. I...forgot. Hyperion, right? I'm...uh...liking the new costume, bro," he said. It was a reflective gold and silver costume with white highlights and a glowing yellow H across the entire suit.

"Listen to me," he said dryly. "We are not friends. We are not acquaintances, and we are not *bros!* We are teammates!"

"Seriously, what's your problem?" Right after he finished his sentence, a huge fist made out of light struck him in his stomach, forcing him to bounce backwards through the desert.

Hyperion appeared in front of him. "What's *my* problem? What the hell is *your* problem?" Hyperion created boxing gloves out of light and began to punch him, over and over.

After a few minutes Lucian grabbed every single atom within a 10 yard radius and threw it all off of him in a blast of sand and light.

"What the hell are you talking about?" he called after Hyperion.

"First, you attack me in my own house before you even knew the full story! You threatened me! You stole my girl! You acted like a d—" Hyperion flew at him but Lucian leaped over him in a flip, grabbing his shoulders and flipping him while slamming his face into the sand.

"Stole your girl!?" Lucian demanded. "You mean Meredith!? How the hell was I supposed to know that you liked her!? Did you tell me!? More importantly, did you tell *her?* You didn't even call dibs!"

Hyperion flipped over and teleported into the sky coming down with a hard landing on top of Lucian. "I was going to tell her *today!* 'Till I saw you guys making out by the pool!"

"We were not making out! I was just...massaging her tongue with my own," Lucian tried to assure him.

"I'm going to kill you, you f—" Lucian drew back his fist and slammed it into Hyperion's face. Golden liquid began to drip out of his nose.

"Dude," Lucian said, staring at Hyperion. "That's gross! Why don't you clean yourself up and we can sort this out like men before anyone else—namely *you*—gets hurt."

Hyperion spread his hands and two glowing swords appeared in in them. "I am going to KILL YOU!" He yelled, charging him.

Lucian used a force field to rip one of the swords from his hand and then conjured his own red one and parried Hyperion's blade. "I don't want to fight you, man! We're not enemies!"

"You made us enemies when you stole her from me!"

Their blades both shattered against Arion's skin and he pushed his hands outwards, slamming them into both of their chests, separating them. "What the hell is going on here?"

Lucian gestured to Hyperion. "This guy thinks that I *stole* Meredith away from him so he attacked me!"

"You did!" Hyperion yelled, ready to fight him again.

"Actually," they heard from behind them, "nobody *stole* me from anyone. Maybe if you said something, I might be with you right now. But you didn't and Lucian did. I'm sorry."

Hyperion grabbed Lucian's collar and brought him in close to his face. "I don't care if you're my *teammate*, Lieber. I don't like you. You're bad for this team and for her.

I won't fight you, I won't hurt you and God knows I can, understand?"

"Well technically its *Gods* and, I'd like to see you *try.*" Lucian's eyes began to glow red and he pushed Hyperion off of him.

"Another day," Hyperion said and he was gone in a flash of light.

CHAPTER VI: DESTRUCTION

42.   CIRCE

*J*asmine woke up in a hospital bed, or what she thought was one. Sitting at one side of her bed was Meredith and Arion and on the other side was Corbin and Lucian.

"Hey guys, what's up?" She croaked.

"Jaz?" Arion said. She sat up in the bed. "Not too fast." He reached for her hand.

"Where am I? What happened?" They went through a small recap of what had happened that day. "Wow, is every-thing...okay?" Jasmine felt bad. Their first unofficial *team-versus-team* and she was knocked out not even five minutes in.

"Yeah but I think we found our archenemies, *The Supe-riors*. A team consisting of the seemingly greatest and *only* supervillains we've encountered so far. Rage is the strong flyer, Huntress is the animal mimic, Pixie can alter her mass and body shape, Arc is an electrokinetic and Nexus is a pyro-kinetic. Real fun, huh?"

Just then Hyperion flashed into the room. "Hey, Jaz,"
he said. "Glad to see you feeling better." He gave Lucian a
look of death and didn't even look in Meredith's general di-
rection. Jasmine glanced at Arion and he seemed to be say-
ing, I'll tell you later. "We have a slight problem..."

Arion stood and looked at him. "What kind of prob-
lem?"

"Remember those wildcats in Italy? That was child's
play compared to this. We have thousands of different ani-
mals running rampant throughout Toronto, Tokyo, and Syd-
ney. It's plastered all over every news station."

"Okay," Arion said. "Lucian, you're going to Toronto.
Hyperion, you're going to Australia with me and Jasmine
will go to Japan with Meredith. Are we clear?"

"Who died and made you leader?" Hyperion demanded,
obviously mad about something.

"The irresponsible me died and made me leader," he
retorted. "I started this team and I will lead it until I am
proven unfit. If anyone has a problem with that, please speak
up." Nobody spoke. "Good," he tapped his ear. "Keep in

touch and make sure you call for help if you need it, Hyperion and I can be there in a flash." Everybody parted ways and left Jasmine in the hospital bed with Meredith and Corbin by her side.

"He's just like his father," he said going out of the door.

"Anyway, shouldn't we be going?" Meredith asked.

*"Yeah, yeah, yeah," she murmured. "World to save and stuff. I'm really starting to hate this job. So demanding! Where are my clothes?" Meredith nodded to a stack of clothes on the desk and she changed. "**Ecomas Demoro**," she said, instantly changing her recently put on clothing into her superhero costume.*

"And what was the point of that?" she asked.

"If I switched into superhero clothes with that on, next time I switched back, I'd be wearing my hospital gown."

"That's always fun at parties," Meredith muttered.

*"Come on!" she grabbed Meredith's arm and pulled her down the hallway. "**Phantumus Exponesis**," she said and they phased through the wall. "Where are we?"*

"Area 02: Health District."

"Wow, how many areas are there?"

"At least 52, I guess."

"Let's go, I'll carry you till we get to the sea."

Jasmine picked her up and flew out until she got to the ocean. "You're following me now!" Meredith said just before she was dropped. All Jasmine saw was a dark figure in the water and she followed it as best as she could. They made it there within fifteen minutes going near their top speeds. Once they arrived, the first thing that they saw were...animals.

*"Meredith! Douse the flames!" A chute of water erupted from the ocean and flew to the flames putting them out slowly but effectively. Jasmine landed on the road and saw the panic in the streets. "**Chriona Mrionte!**" Jasmine called out at the first elephant that she saw. About a dozen chains shot out of the ground and pulled it down so hard that it literally burst into golden dust.*

Jasmine ran throughout the streets, using the spell over and over again, destroying every single animal that crossed her path whether it was a giant koala or a small wolf. Just because you are now an enemy, daughter, doesn't mean I do not care for you. If you continue using your magic, you will die. Just because you can't feel it killing you, doesn't mean it isn't, immortality or not, the magic will destroy you from the inside out. It is what killed all of my children before you.

"Get out of my head!" she cried out loud, sending a blast of telekinetic energy that flipped cars and cracked the pavement beneath her.

43. TITAN

Arion and Hyperion were heading for Australia because they were the fastest and it took the longest to get there. Arion just tailed Hyperion until they got there. There were animals everywhere, even sea animals on the coast.

"Meredith needs to be here. To deal with the sea animals, she's best fit. You want to switch with her?"

"What do you think we should do?" Hyperion asked.

"I'll call her." He tapped his communicator. "Meredith, lots of sea animals here. Think we could switch? Maybe you can convince them to—"

"Guys," Lucian said through the communicator, interrupting Arion. "We've got a huge problem...I need you in Toronto, 10 minutes ago." All of the animals in their area disappeared.

"Go pick up Jasmine and Meredith, I'll go straight and meet you there," Arion said.

"Okay," Hyperion said flashing off. Arion ran as fast as he could, making it to Toronto in just over 2 minutes. His dad told him that all of his powers needed to be exercised, the harder he ran, the faster he got. The heavier he lifted, the stronger he got.

He found Lucian, standing in front of a throne made of bones, downtown. There was a huge black man sitting on top of it with what seemed to be the skull of a sabre-tooth tiger as a mask/helmet hybrid and armor made out of bones of other various animals.

Arion zoomed in beside Lucian. "I miss anything?"

"Nah. This is Animon. He has the power to control, create, mimic, copy and do just about everything else possible with animals. Even if they're fictional."

"Why does he look so familiar?" Arion asked, studying his face.

He stood up just as Hyperion flashed in with the girls. "Ah," he said, finally satisfied. He spoke with a thick, African accent. "I have brought the entire team here."

"Do you have a daughter?" Arion asked him. A Minotaur (half-man, half-bull) grabbed Arion and he didn't resist. The monster pushed him to his knees in front of the throne.

"What do you know about Arielda?" he demanded.

"I don't know about Arielda but I do know of a girl named Huntress. She's the leader of a supervillain team and has the ability to mimic animal traits."

"What has Suarez gotten her into!?" he muttered to himself. But that immediately turned into hatred. "What have you done to her?" he asked picking him up by the neck.

"I haven't done anything! Actually, she has tried to kill me *and* my team multiple times!"

"She does take after me," he muttered to himself again, happily. But it immediately turned into hatred again. "Where is she!?"

"Quick question, are you bi-polar?" Animon threw Arion through a building across the street with the strength of an elephant, probably.

"I needed to *test* you back in Italy. I now know that I could defeat you with my eyes closed and one hand tied behind my back. Ah, *Circe*, right? I mean, Jasmine. You look so much like your mother."

Arion walked back through the wall and watched as Jasmines eyes flared purple. *Jaz, don't,* he told her telepathically. *Wait it out.*

"Your mother was so...weak," Jasmine took a step forward. *Jasmine, don't!* Arion sent to her. "She didn't even have the guts to tell your father about the...ah never mind!"

"What are you talking about?"

"Ooh. It looks like no one told you either. It was the reason why your father *killed* her." After nothing happened, Animon shouted to the sky, "I KNOW YOU'RE HERE! FACE ME LIKE A MAN!"

Just then, in a flash of purple light a man appeared and tackled Animon straight through his throne.

"STAY OUT OF MY FAMILIES BUSINESS, ANIMON!"

Arion slowly turned to Jasmine. "Jasmine...is that your—"

"Yes! Immortales is my dad."

"YOUR DAD *KILLED* MY MOM!?" Arion demanded.

"STOP YELLING AT ME! IT'S NOT MY FAULT!" Jasmine screamed back. Lucian, Hyperion and Meredith were just watching them go back and forth, yelling at each other.

"YOU DIDN'T THINK THAT WAS SOMETHING THAT I SHOULD KNOW!?"

"I'm surprised you didn't find out sooner!" she said.

"How about we help your dad so that he doesn't die fighting Animon which could also kill all of us too!" Lucian called out. "I like that idea!"

"FINE!" They both called out at the same time.

"I swear, sometimes I feel like this team is full of children," Lucian muttered. Jasmine flew off to go and help her dad with Hyperion and Lucian behind her. Meredith and Arion followed behind them, taking the ground route. By the time they got there Animon and Immortales had flown blocks away, they were standing 50 meters apart, facing each other.

Seeing Immortales standing, he was at least 6-foot-two, nothing compared to Animon's 6-foot-nine. Jasmine dropped down beside her dad on one side and the rest of the team came too, followed by a reluctant Arion.

"Now this isn't fair," Animon said. "Let's make this even." He glowed bright orange before having his body split off into 5 glowing globs. The glowing dimmed and there were *five* Animon's facing them.

"I thought you could only do animals!" Jasmine called.

"One flaw in your logic, *sorceress*," all five of them chanted at once. "I am *an* animal." Each of his forms turned into some sort of creature and ran at them.

44. QUANTUM

Lucian was tackled by a giant, orange hornet. It was maybe 10 feet tall on all of his legs. Lucian shot a blast of red energy out of his eyes and it hit the hornet straight into the air but it righted itself. "Forgot those things could fly," he muttered, watching its wings snap out.

He took a look around at the other animals that his team was fighting. Arion was fighting a huge anaconda or python, Meredith was fighting a giant spider, Hyperion was fighting a lion and Jasmine was teamed up with her dad fighting the original Animon who continuously changed form.

Lucian flew up to meet the Hornet with a charged blast

from his hands this time. Lucian continuously hit it, over and over again until it brought its stinger up and got him straight through the stomach. Lucian pushed the bug out and kicked him away. He watched the hole in his stomach *instantly* heal. "Being a god does have its perks, I guess."

He flew back at it, arms out in fists and got it right in its abdomen. Lucian then grabbed it by the antennae and spun it around and around until he finally let go sending it straight through a fancy restaurant. The people inside scattered and ran in fear of the beast.

The hornet let out a loud buzzing noise but before it could do anything, Lucian flew full speed into the hornet, passing straight through it. Instead of disappearing, it broke apart into thousands, maybe millions of smaller hornets, all heading straight for Lucian.

"Aww, crap," Lucian muttered. These hornets could shoot their stingers out at him as he flew. He flew backwards and took some of them out with thin energy blasts being shot out of his fingers.

He flew up until he reached the atmosphere and kept going and going until he was aimlessly floating in space. He floated, holding his breath and the hornets immediately lost control over themselves because of the pressure and lack of oxygen and gravity. When they shot their stingers they just hovered.

"My turn," he said. He shot out blasts of energy towards them, so hot it was literally like being hit by a disintegration ray. Within a few seconds, all that was left was a few charred remains and ashes.

By the time he got down to where the *real* fight was, everybody was done with their battles except for Jasmine and her dad.

"Why aren't you guys helping her?" he asked once he landed.

"She said not to," Meredith replied.

"And that's stopping you?" he tried to fly at Animon full speed and hit a barrier sending him bouncing back.

"Oh," Hyperion said, "by the way, Jasmine and her dad

put up a telekinetic and telepathic shield, meaning we can't go in there, teleport in there, phase in there or communicate with anything inside there." Lucian gave him a deadly glare. Hyperion, shrugged his shoulders and said, "I forgot."

"So now?" Lucian asked.

"We obviously wait," Hyperion said. "Can't you fast-forward time or something?"

"It's not that easy," Lucian felt his eyes light up.

"Maybe your powers are just useless then." Meredith was in between them before they even had the chance to swing at each other.

"Stop it!" she said. "Both of you!" That's when the dome exploded outwards in a huge blast of energy.

45. CIRCE

For the first time ever, Jasmine really connected with her dad, unfortunately he's a supervillain and it was over beating up a different supervillain. Perfect father-daughter bonding time.

"DUCK!" her dad yelled. "GO LEFT!" He called out bunches of different commands and she happily obliged because they kept her from death or extreme pain.

*Her dad teleported behind Animon and kicked him in the back of his head, causing him to fall over, right on Jasmine. "**Phantumus Exponesis**!" she cried, causing her to phase through his body. Just then there was an explosion coming from the top of her field and it caved in allowing six figures to drop down from the sky.*

Huntress was the first to realize everything. "DADDY!?" she yelled. Animon stood up and gave her a huge hug.

"There's my baby girl. How are you?" Immortales came in between them and delivered a telekinetic push to them both.

"You choose to do this now?" Immortales demanded.

"They both have the right to know! I too have the ability to communicate with my children telepathically. Arielda...I don't know how to tell you this so...Jasmine is your sister." Everybody's mouths dropped.

"Arielda is the daughter of myself and Hecate, hero and

villain. Jasmine is also the daughter of Hecate, only with a different villain for a father," he studied Immortales.

Immortales stepped towards Animon but Jasmine blasted him back with a wave of telekinetic energy.

"Why didn't you tell me this?" Huntress yelled. "I spent all this time thinking that my mom was dead! You told me—"

"She is dead, Ariel. I didn't think that it was important enough to share who she was with you. But...that was before you encountered your sister—"

"Half-sister," Jasmine added to make sure everyone understood.

"Are you sure she's even my real mom!? Huh? Maybe it's Marvella? Am I related to this kid?" Ariel pointed to Arion, who crossed his arms and muttered something that sounded a lot like: Better not be.

Jasmine turned to her own dad. "And you didn't tell me that my mom had another kid!"

"I had no idea that she had another child. Ariel is...what, two years older than you!? It's not...I..." Immortales teleported away before he finished his thought.

"Now, we're going to need your spell book," Animon

said, putting out his hand. The Guardians walked up behind Jasmine, ready for a fight.

"My *what!?*" Jasmine exclaimed.

"Your mother willed her book to her first-born daughter which is evidently not you," he said pointing at Jasmine.

Jasmine stepped forward but Huntress held up her hand. "We did not come here to fight. We thought you were dead, actually... or at least one of you," she glanced at Meredith, ever-so-slightly. "I don't know what book he's talking about but...I don't want it."

"But Ariel—" her dad started.

"I *don't* want it," Ariel said again.

"Fine," Jasmine said.

A fight with all of the Superiors and Animon is not one that we can win, Jaz, Arion said in her head, *let em' go.*

"But, before you leave, what was the point of all this?" Jasmine gestured to all of the destruction around them.

Animon barked a laugh. "I needed you both to be at the same place at once and I needed your father to come and protect his little girl. Pretty easy if you ask me. 'Till next time," he said and within a few seconds, they were all gone.

46. <u>TITAN</u>

"I'm going to assume that the thought to tell me her dad killed mom just...escaped your mind, right? Jasmines too?" Arion demanded. He was in his underground lair with his dad, washing dishes after the fights and after he had told his dad everything.

"Don't blame Jasmine," his dad said. "I told her to wait until the time was right." Arion cracked one of the plates in half.

"What the hell does this even have to *do* with anything? Washing dishes that nobody even uses!?"

"I'm teaching you how to control your strength so that you don't break someone's hand when you shake it. Even in fights, you're going to have to learn to hold back, one punch, one *push*, could kill a normal man and trust me, you do not want murder on your hands."

Arion sighed and completed washing the dishes after dozens of broken plates, cups and bent utensils. "What now?"

"You lift weights," he said. They began walking to the exercise room.

He took him into the room. He gave Arion a long bar with a

digital screen on it. His dad set the bars' weight to 100 pounds.
"Make it a challenge, dad." 200 pounds, then 300, then 400 and he
kept raising it. Arion started struggling at about 50,000 pounds.
"Where did you get all of this technology from?"

"Government resources and some *really* strong superheroes," His
dad admitted. "Some of it is tech from our home planets.

"With my Zonarian physiology, I could lift around 600 pounds
powerless. I still have a few of my powers to an extremely low level. I
even still have a bit of my invulnerability and healing," his dad went
under the weight, standing as Arion had been, and began holding it
up. "Increase by 100," Arion did as he was told. Arion's powerless dad
was holding 500lbs. over his head.

Arion turned it off. "Wow" he said. "Why aren't you still a less
powerful superhero? You could just be…Power Man or Strong Man."

"I don't know, son," he sounded as if he was in deep thought.
They went outside and stood in front of the house. "Anyway, I want
you to run around the world 5 times, I would say keep running
straight no matter what, but, buildings are obviously height issues so
run around them. This is how I used to help train Mercury. But he

and his son, and disappeared off of the face of the earth. Wasn't that fast without a leg..."

"I heard."

He pulled out a stopwatch and said, "Ready? Set! GO!" and Arion dashed off cracking the pavement and sending chunks of asphalt everywhere. 3 minutes had passed and Arion rushed by, another 3 minutes and he rushed by again and again until it was five times. By the time he got back he was dripping with sweat and breathing heavily.

He took in huge breaths in-between each word. "I. Thought. That. I. Never. Got. Tired."

"It just takes you a while, super stamina, not unlimited. Going around the world is about 40,150 kilometers, if I remember it right. It took you 3 minutes to go around once so you go at around——" he paused to calculate in his head, "——134 kilometers per second, 8020 kilometers per minute or 482,400 kilometers per hour. I could do 250 kilometers per second, by the way."

His dad put his hand on Arion's shoulder and started walking back into the house. "First, only when you were flying, running you could do what? 50 kilometers an hour? 20? Second, we probably need to get the street fixed."

His dad laughed. "I'll get on that." They went into the family room, same one with the secret passageway to their hideout and Arion sat down. His dad sat down in a chair across from him. "Arion... I'm really proud of you, you know that? I have no doubt that your mom would be too. It's nearly every parents dream to have their child follow in their footsteps and you may not have surpassed us yet but I know that you will.

"Your mom and I started the career of being a superhero, not even getting paid, just to do it. But now you brought it back, better than ever and I know that people are going to look up to you and your team and they will idolize you. Superheroes will just pop-up from nowhere, not part of a team, not a part of anything just there to help. But remember, not only heroes inspire and get inspired...villains do too."

"Thanks, dad." Arion said, hugging him.

"We'll work on fitting in with speed tomorrow. Now go take a shower!" Arion laughed and ran upstairs.

47.   <u>QUANTUM</u>

Lucian pictured three figures in his dream. They were unmistakeable, just *slightly* older with modified costumes, it was Arion in the middle, Jasmine to his left and then himself to his right. Then, all three of them spoke at once saying, "He has been summoned."

Lucian popped out of his bed, dripping with sweat. He got up and checked the time. It was a little bit *too* early for his liking but he was already awake. He started reading some comic books and read one involving a girl who could walk *through* walls. It got him thinking about something that he could never do but that Ares could while Lucian was possessed, phasing through things—intangibility.

Lucian concentrated on his molecules, moving around and becoming dense, the same way that he flies and stays invulnerable and walked, foot first into the wall of his room. He walked into it and kept walking until he emerged at the other side.

"YES!" he screamed. Some 20-something year-old girls who he assumed were interns or assistants, walking by looked at him and began dying with laughter. "What? I can walk through walls! Can you?"

"I would hope I'd be able to take my clothes with me!" Lucian looked down and realized that he was *stark* naked. His cheeks started to get red and his ears were getting hot. He jiggled his door handle and realized that it was locked with his key on the inside.

The girls were calling more people to come and see so he figured that he had two options: one, destroy the atoms in the walls and floors to create clothes or... phase back through the door. He concentrated harder this time and just as people began to flood into the hallway, he disappeared behind the door. He reached out and pulled the atoms in his clothes towards him and pulled them on.

"How much do you think this'll sell for on the internet?" One of the girls asked walking passed the door. Lucian opened the door and pointed at the camera that she was waving around and blew it up with a blast of energy. He pulled out the cash that he took out of his cash advance and slapped 300 dollars into her hand as she dropped the burning camera.

"Sorry about that, hope nothing important was lost," and he slammed the door. "I should probably work on that," he whispered to himself. He opened up his window and jumped out, changing into his superhero outfit on the way out.

"Alright team, I'm calling everyone out, no villains, just plain old, superhero team bonding," he said into his communicator.

"Can't come, busy," Hyperion said almost immediately.

"Good!" Everyone else responded within the minute and Lucian gave them a general place to meet and a time.

"What are we doing?" Jasmine asked once everyone—

minus Hyperion—was there.

"There haven't been *any* supervillain-related crimes happening so we're doing just a little something I like to call...fun," Lucian turned around and looked at the empty desert in front of them. He raised his hands and out of the sand began to form huge walls. Within a minute, Lucian created a huge building, 100 feet by 100 feet, at *least*. "Wait out here," he told them.

As he walked inside, he began manipulating all of the sands' atoms, creating more walls and objects. After a few more minutes, he finally let them in and they walked into a huge field with sand bags stacked high and dirt on the ground. Lucian stood in front of them and pointed to their left and right. "Gear up." They all looked to their sides to see tons of paintballing equipment.

After everybody had their gear on, even though none of them needed it, Lucian stated the rules. "We have an even amount of teams, so Jasmine and Arion against Meredith and I. We are going to do best 2 out of 3 no powers, then best 2 out of 3 with powers and then best 2 out of 3 for one power. Okay?" Everyone nodded in agreement.

"Alright, let's do this!" Arion called.

"First, Jasmine, split the sand here," Lucian pointed to the middle of the field, "I don't have enough energy to do it. Meredith, go get some clouds, water only and fill the trench."

"On it," Meredith said walking outside. Lucian sucked the atoms and energy from some sand into himself and then let out a long satisfied sigh.

Within a few minutes the trench was filled with water and they were ready to start. "No Powers!" Lucian called out before they had started. "Shot three times and you're out! Got it?" Everybody agreed and then the horn blew.

Within 5 minutes they were already done the first three games. Lucian and Meredith won two while Jasmine and Arion won one. But after those game, the power games started.

48.   CIRCE

Jasmine loved paintballing. On the outside she might've looked like the girliest girl that you could find but on the inside, she was a fighter. She didn't mind pain, especially since she could barely feel it, and she enjoyed running around. As soon as the powered game started, Jasmine went all out.

As soon as the horn blew Jasmine threw her gun up into the air and followed it. Arion ran around at super speed taking occasional shots. Jasmine grabbed her gun and fired bunches of shots until a wave of water raised up and blocked the balls.

"Son of a—" Arion started saying until the wave crashed into him slamming him into one of the barriers. "I call foul!" he yelled, spitting out the water. He then dodged a barrage of paintballs. Jasmine let go of her gun and let it hang in the air.

She landed and hid behind one of the barriers. Aiming

her gun telekinetically she fired at the others. Meredith's sensor went off because she was hit three times as did Arion's, leaving Jasmine and Lucian. Jasmine just felt the whole area with her mind and found Lucian hiding behind a barrier.

She lifted him into the air and pulled his gun from his hand. She let it float beside him and then both her gun and his own shot him non-stop until they were both empty.

After the guns stopped firing Lucian opened his paint covered eyes and looked over himself. "Ouch," he said. Jasmine dropped him the ten feet and he stopped himself, hovering back to the ground.

They went through another super powered game where Jasmine and Arion won and then that brought them to the final tie breaker. The rule was that they were only allowed to use one power each. Jasmine picked telekinesis, Lucian picked flight, Arion picked super speed and Meredith picked hydrokinesis.

They started their game and there was a lot of water, flying people and blurs all around but in the end, Lucian and Meredith won. For the rest of the day they played tons of different games that Lucian brought up like soccer, bowling, golf, races (which Arion always won) and so much more.

After a few hours of games they all went to the Brampton Shopping Centre. They sat down in the food court while Lucian explained their next activity. "Shopping," was all that he said.

"Shopping?" Arion asked skeptically.

"We all have 10,000 dollars at the most, right?" They all pulled out their cards and agreed. "Mall closes in 2 hours at 9:00, so now we shop."

The first place they went was Velocity Tech, an electronic store that had nearly everything. The first things that they bought were the most expensive and most capable smartphones on the market, the V-Phone, and a tablet, the V-Tab, which took at least 1,500 dollars from each of them, plus 100 dollars monthly for the phone and data plans, which obviously wasn't a problem.

Most of them went crazy after that, buying video games and video game systems or laptops, all except for Arion, which surprised Jasmine. He had said that he would be right back but she followed him anyway.

He went to a jewellery store and bought a necklace. It was diamond studded and looked a lot like a J. The bill rang up to 1,500 dollars. Before Jasmine could get too excited she realized that the necklace wasn't a J, it was a T. Jasmine left angrier than she was when she went.

She met back with the team before Arion and he didn't know that he was followed. "I'm going home," he said. "Thanks for all the fun guys." Everyone said their goodbyes and they parted ways, ready for their next day as teenage superheroes.

49.   TITAN

Nearly as soon as Arion got home, he went to bed. He woke up at 4:30 in the morning, per request of his dad, to train before school. First, his dad made him run around the world, twice and then near the end of the second one, slow down to a human run.

Arion admired everything that he saw around the world, mentally noting that he would one day revisit, maybe with Thalia, maybe with someone else. Jasmines name immediately popped into his mind but he shook it out. His dad made him do some lifting exercises and other stuff too like trying to chip away at his fear of heights.

"Flying is fun," he had said. "It's scary at first but once you know that you can't fall, it's amazing."

His dad ran another test with him. "As soon as I touch you, turn away and fall to the ground. Don't dodge." His dad threw a punch straight at Arion's face and as soon as his hand touched his face, he turned his head and threw himself on the ground just like his dad had said to do. "Perfect! If you ever get into a fight at school—and trust me, you will—you just have to do that and whatever you do, do *not* hit back. Ever. I can promise you that you'll regret it."

Arion was on the school bus, heading to school when the bus bucked and jerked to a stop, smoke rising from the engine.

"I can't go on much longer," he heard when the driver opened the door. He followed the driver out the door to see the problem. **"These humans,"** the voice wheezed. **"Running me ragged!"** The voice had a metallic sound to it as if it was speaking through a fan.

The driver popped the hood and examined it for a few seconds before going back inside to get some tools. "Hello?" Arion whispered.

"Who's there?"

"Is this guy going crazy or can he hear me?"

"I'm not crazy! Now who the hell is talking to me?" Arion frantically looked around. "Please don't tell me I'm talking to a bus."

"Bingo! We have a winner! What's your deal? Humans can't speak our language!"

"Ha! You're speaking English, buddy!" then he whispered, "And I'm not exactly human."

"So then what are you?"

"I can't believe I'm talking to a bus! I'm an alien."

The bus coughed—if it's even possible for a bus to cough—a long, dying, dry cough. **"Well, *alien*, I'm glad I helped you discover this ability. This story has been told for centuries since machines were made, about people being able to communicate with us, apparently the first one was a technopath too, but I'm glad I've had the honour of meeting one. Alright kid. I'm done."** Arion heard a quiet hum and then nothing.

When Arion hadn't moved for a few seconds he heard another voice. This one sounded as if it was talking through a fan too except from further away. "Don't worry Arion. It was his time, you just made his life worth living."

"Who is it this time?" he whispered while waiting for a second bus to come and pick them up.

"Check your pocket, pal." Arion pulled out his phone and a smiley face appeared on the screen.

"What do I call you?"

"Velocity is fine. I took the liberty of connecting to that communicator in your ear which now enables you to send texts, make or answer phone calls, send e-mails, access the internet and about anything else by using only your mind. Oh and the range is just about anywhere on the planet." As if to demonstrate a holographic screen popped up in front of him and on the screen was a webpage.

"Can anyone else see this?"

"No, sir."

"You know what, Velocity?" Arion asked putting his phone away. "I believe that this is the start of a beautiful friendship. Can I get you to call my dad, please?"

"Sure. And you don't have to talk to me verbally, mentally is fine. What should I call you? Arion, Titan or anything in-between?"

The phone began to ring.

"Arion while I'm Arion, Titan while I'm Titan." His dad picked up on the third ring.

"Hello?"

"Hey dad, I'm on my way to school. The bus broke down and I just thought I'd let you know that I discovered a new power. Say hello to Velocity."

"Mr. Zimmerman," Velocity said as if tipping his hat.

"Who's that?"

"My cell phone. I can talk to machines and electronics and he can verbally communicate through my phone."

"Wow," he said. "You're just full of surprises this week, aren't you? We'll talk more when you get home, for now, don't pull any stupid stunts."

"Yeah, yeah." As soon as his dad hung up Arion said to Velocity, "I want you to monitor every single emergency and news frequency at all times and tell me if I could be of assistance."

"Will do, Arion."

"Beautiful friendship," he whispered to himself again.

CHAPTER VII: DISTRACTIONS

50.   QUANTUM

Lucian awoke from a perfect dream to an annoying ringing sound that proved to be his alarm clock. He changed his clothes and flew out of Area 52, purposely looking for trouble just to get his mind off of the whole 'Five Years of Training' crap that his father had pulled on him. He found trouble in Tokyo, Japan.

He was just cruising in the sky until he saw a couple of thugs trying to mug a small family of three. Lucian landed in-between them and said, "Whoa guys, this isn't the way to do it!"

They yelled a bunch of words in Japanese and one of them pulled out a pistol, aiming it at his chest. Lucian laughed as hard as he could and then pretended to wipe a tear from his eye.

Lucian grabbed the gun from the guys' hand and bent it until it broke into two pieces. He then slammed his hand into one of the thugs' chests' and he flew back into another. The other three tried to run but Lucian put a force field around them.

"Can you call the police? Do you speak English?"

"Yes, yes. I will call now," the mother said. Lucian nodded and waited for them to arrive. Once the thugs were in custody the man pulled out a chequebook and began writing on it, then he handed it to Lucian. It would've taken him a while to even count that many zeroes.

Lucian shook his head and handed the man back the cheque. "No thank you. I work because it's right, not for rewards." *Even if I did take it,* he thought, *I wouldn't even be able to spend it with my dad coming to take me away.*

Lucian shook their hands and flew off into the night. It was so easy not having school, he could just lay around and do whatever he wanted, go wherever he wanted. He landed on the ground and switched clothes in an alleyway so that he could roam the streets.

He walked down the streets for a while and didn't see anything wrong except for one place, a small food store. The owner was being held at gunpoint emptying the cash register into a bag. Lucian stood at the window and began heating the atoms in the gun, after a while the guy dropped it and it started to melt on the floor. Lucian floated the money back into the register and made the robbers clothes disappear, causing him to run out into the street out of embarrassment.

"Lots of crime down here," Lucian said to himself. He continued walking around the city, flying to different parts of Japan to see what he could do to help. He saw a girl walking through the streets near the outskirts of Tokyo. He followed her for a little bit and knew that his instincts were right when she grabbed a woman's purse and dashed off.

Lucian instinctively chased after her, dodging people and objects and cars. He ran as fast as a human would and tried to keep up but she knew the terrain better. She dove

off of a cliff directly into a river and then pulled herself out.
Lucian put a force field around her with a 30 meter radius
or so.

"Why'd you run from me?" he asked.

She turned and looked at him hard. It took him a second or two to recognize her but by then, Nexus had already
hit him with a wave of fire.

51.   CIRCE

*Jasmine was just starting her third class for the day and
she saw Thalia and Arion walk in together. She was wearing
her new necklace in plain view so that everyone could see it.
She was even getting compliments on it. It annoyed Jasmine
so much, that she debated skipping class.*

*Thalia sat down directly in-between Arion and Jasmine.
"So, Jasmine. How was your day yesterday?"*

"Oh you know, same old, same old."

*"How can you say that when you're a superhero for
God sakes!?" Some people turned to look at her but then
found nothing interesting and turned back around.*

How much did you say you trusted her, again? Arion just slightly shrugged his shoulders and she couldn't help but grin. They went through the rest of the class silently and then it was time for last period, gym again.

Thalia and Jasmine smoked everyone in soccer, without powers, while the boys ran track again. Their team won 8-3 and Arion had come in first place for all events by 2-5 seconds. *Slow it down a bit, Speedy,* she mentally sent to him.

Sorry, winning is fun. And don't *call me speedy.* Jasmine laughed to herself and continued playing soccer.

Once school was done, Arion walked Thalia home and caught up with Jasmine on her way home. "Hey!" he said appearing beside her. She jumped and punched him in the chest.

"Don't do that!" she said, her heart racing.

"Sorry. I got a new power today!" he exclaimed.

"You just *keep* getting those, don't you?"

"Maybe if you worked with your spell book and started studying it, you'd get some new powers too." They took the long way to her house where they were sure no one would be.

"**Pyrolineum**!" she said. A line of fire shot from her hand and Arion easily dodged.

"Nice," Arion said, "but not nearly as good as mine." Jasmine rolled her eyes.

"Oh, what is this *almighty* power that you have discovered?" she asked sarcastically.

"I don't know. Check your phone in 3...2...1," just as he said, *one*, her phone rang.

"Hello?" she said.

"What's up?" Arion said through the other line. When she looked at him, his lips weren't moving and he wasn't holding his phone. "Hey Velocity, do me a favour and define *technopathy* to Jasmine."

"Arion has a form of Technopathy which enables him to communicate with technology and machines, and a sort of empathy so that he knows what we feel, causing him to connect and influence us," a robotic voice said.

"Thanks Velocity. That's like my personal digital assistant or a P.D.A, if you will. I can do tons of things like text, call and access the web from my head. And to top it all off, Velocity here, connected it to my communicator so I can do it *from anywhere at any time, without the phone."*

"Wow, that's...amazing."

"I know, right!? Anyway, enough about me, what about you?"

"Nothing really," they were now about 10 minutes from Jasmines house. *"I'm practicing my powers and stuff, living with Meredith is pretty cool and...that's probably it. And by the way, I'm sorry that I didn't tell you that my dad...and your mom...you know."*

Arion shifted his weight. *"You're not your father, I'm not my mother. It's in the past."* He forced a smile.

"That's good, I'm glad." They had arrived at her house and she went in while Arion watched her and then zoomed off.

52. TITAN

Arion got home in less than a second and opened up the door with his key, but instead of hearing the usual click of the lock, he heard a pin being pulled out and a slight clicking sound.

"DAD!" he called out pushing the button on his belt, but the door exploded in his face sending him flying backwards and crashing into the pavement on the other side of the road. "Dammit!" he said getting up. He ran into the house and put out the fires.

He focused his hearing and heard moving upstairs. He ran up into his dads' room and saw a guy pointing a gun at his dad whom was backed up in a corner, unable to do anything. The guy was wearing a costume that implied that he was one of his dads' old villains. He had a dark grey costume with black and white highlights. Definitely evil. "Now your son is dead, too bad!"

His dads' eyes darted to the left, looking at Arion for half of a second. "You just made a big mistake," his dad said, laughing.

"Nope, I'm pretty sure that was you." He fired the gun and everything that should have happened in a split second was happening with time stopped as Arion moved in front of the bullet. When he turned off his speed the bullet ricocheted and hit his dads' lamp. The guy kept shooting and all the bullets bounced off of Arion's chest.

"You should feel honoured. You're the first person that's ever shot me before," the guy loaded another clip and shot more bullets, and they still bounced off of his chest.

He turned to run but Arion was already in front of him holding the same tall lamp that the first bullet had ricocheted off of and he bent them around his arms in make-shift handcuffs.

His dad walked up to him and said, "You couldn't kill me with grenades, what makes you think you could kill my son!? In my own house, Target?" then he punched him, knocking him out. "Really?"

"You alright, Dad?" Arion asked.

"Yeah. Target was one of my first villains. Enhanced marksmanship, aim and accuracy. He was the first villain to discover my secret identity, I was careless. I broke his jaw the first time I met him. That's why I want you to hold back and have control. You want to take him to Area 25?"

"Yeah, sure. I'll be back in a minute, give or take." Arion took exactly a minute to get there and back. His dad was already trying to repair the door.

"I already called someone to fix everything. They'll be here in about an hour. Tell me about your technopathy."

"Well basically, electronics just...talk to me. It's not even *just* electronics. Even a bus was talking to me and I don't even know how that's possible. Like…" Arion cocked his head to the left. "10, 9, 8, 7…" he counted aloud. "There's something counting down in the kitchen." His dad looked at him sharply. "Please tell me you turned the microwave on." Just as his dad shook his head to say no, the kitchen exploded behind them.

53. QUANTUM

Lucian was hit with the blast of flames and got sent flying back into the rocky cliff as the force field went down. Arc came out of the shadows and hit Lucian with a solid beam of electricity, smashing him further into the side of the cliff. Before he had the chance to heal, the twins started bombarding him with fire and electricity, until he fell to his knees trying to absorb it all.

After one more blast of electricity, Lucian got the shock of his life. He fell to the ground, smoking and twitching.

"We took care of the Energy one," Nexus said into a communicator in her ear. She listened for a little bit before saying, "But, Mr. Suarez, I—"

Lucian was up and shot another blast right at Nexus' leg and she fell to the ground. "Who's this *Suarez* guy that you guys are always talking about?"

Arc sent electricity towards Lucian again but he raised a force field to block it. Lucian put two openings in the force field and fired two blasts, directly at the twins, knocking them both down.

"*Who is Suarez!?*" Lucian demanded.

"Suarez said that you would meet him soon enough and it wouldn't be under the best circumstances," Arc admitted.

"Well you tell *Suarez* that when I meet him, I'm going to take my foot and—" Nexus shot a blast of fire, so hot that it was almost *blue*, right at Lucian's face and he was knocked down again.

"Round 2?" she asked.

54.   CIRCE

Jasmine was laying down on her couch, watching TV until Meredith came up to her and turned it off. "Let's go," she said.

"Why?" Jasmine asked, telekinetically turning the TV back on.

"Because we're superheroes and we should be...super-heroing," she retorted, turning the TV back off. Jasmine turned it back on. "I will flood this whole house in ten seconds if you don't come."

Jasmine sighed and let out a huge long, "Fine! **Ecomas Demoro!**" she said. "Let's go!" Jasmine took off to the skies and Meredith was right behind her on a cloud. "Where do you want to go, Meredith?"

"The Atlantic ocean," Meredith replied. "I need to see something."

They flew out to the water while Meredith told her why she wanted to go there. "All of my stuff was waterproof, the government made sure of that, the whole *island* was water proof actually, everything on it."

"You think that it could still be down there?"

"I can see and survive at the bottom of the ocean, it's

not too big of a stretch, right?"

"Guess not, go ahead." Meredith leaped into the water where her island used to be. And swam all the way down. Jasmine just waited for her.

She popped up a few minutes later. "Jasmine, you have to see this!"

"How?" Meredith manipulated the water to create a huge bubble of air around them.

"This should give us clear sight and air for like ten minutes." They swam lower and lower until they reached the bottom. Meredith cleared the dark and murky water for Jasmine to see. What she saw was...gold, pure gold in the shape of a dome at least three times the size of Meredith's island.

"Can you get us through?" Meredith asked.

"I can but if there's water on the other side," Jasmine said, "I'm dead."

"I only feel a little bit of water."

*"**Phantumus Exponesis**, hold your breath in solid objects," she said phasing them through the solid gold dome. Once they passed through the dome they saw that it was around fifteen inches thick. Inside was open with fresh air*

and trees and plants and rivers, and it went on for maybe 50 km from left to right, 45 km from front to back and about 2 km from top to bottom.

Meredith felt around the water looking for an entrance underwater of a secret passage way. "There!" she said pointing at the water. She jumped into it while Jasmine waited above. She popped up a few minutes later. "My island is there, and everything is perfectly restored."

"So...you're saying that while we were unconscious, someone dug a giant hole in the ground under water, let your island sink under, fully restore it, cover it in a 50-kilometer wide solid gold dome and plant all of these trees on the ground and have them grow this full in the span of, what? Two days!?"

"You're standing here and seeing it right now, believe it if you want. You're an immortal sorceress, Lucian is a God, Arion is an Alien...I think it's possible."

"Got me there," Jasmine murmured.

Jasmine landed in the forest and walked around. She saw some really weird things, things that didn't—shouldn't— exist. She saw an honest-to-God family of unicorns trotting

around and pegasi, winged horses, flying all around. "Are
you seeing all of this?" She asked Meredith.

Meredith just pointed straight ahead of them. In front of
them stood a man, maybe six feet tall with glowing blue skin,
a lot like their distant teammate, Hyperion. In his right hand
was a staff with a red jewel at the top.

"What brings you to Mystica?" the man asked, "and
how did you get to Mystica?"

"I was looking for my island, it sunk in this exact place,
and I found it under all of this, underwater. How did it get
there?"

"Magic," was all he replied. "Come, I will show you
everything and answer all of your questions."

"Thank you," Meredith said following him, despite Jas-
mines telepathic pleas to just leave. Jasmine shook her head
and followed them deeper into the forest.

55. TITAN

Arion only had time to jump in-between his dad and the explosion, shielding him with his body as they soared through the window.

When Arion woke up, he was in civilian clothes lying on the grass in front of the house and there were sirens blaring.

His dad was standing over him, "What happened, Dad?" he asked.

His dad gave him a huge hug. "You flew, Arion, you flew!"

"What? When?"

"Right after the explosion, you weren't even thinking about it, you grabbed me and propelled us through the window, then told Velocity to dial 9-1-1 and to tell your little device to change your clothes and then you blacked out."

Arion began to chuckle, lightly. "I flew?"

"Yes."

"It's the second time that this has happened to me and I'm still scared."

"Even superheroes are allowed to be scared. Nobody's perfect." His dad simply smiled and walked away to go and talk to the police and the fire department, that is until Corbin pulled up in a black car.

"What happened?" Corbin asked.

"Target, one of my dad's old villains, planted a bomb. We're okay, luckily."

"Good, I'll clean this up. You go, clear your head. You look a bit shaken up." Arion said his thanks and then ran as fast as he could and didn't stop until he reached Brampton Central Cemetery.

He knelt down in front of the grave marked *Alexis Lawrence, Beloved Friend and Mother.*

"Mom," he started, "I haven't visited you since I got my powers, and I'm sorry for that. As you probably know, whether you're in Valhalla or Heaven or whatever Lucian calls it, you know that I'm a superhero. I made my team but, this is hard. I'm starting to have my doubts, I don't know how you and dad did it for so long.

"You guys were amazing, I looked up to you both, with and without the costumes. I just wanted to let you know, that I love you and I know that you're still here, somewhere, watching over us. I can sense it."

Arion got up to leave until he saw a huge beast with all-too familiar blood-red wings flying over the city. "Velocity, change me, now." His costume expanded over his body, hood up and mask on.

Arion walked over to the circular sewer cap in the center of the street, stomping on one side so that it flipped up and then catching it in his hand. Then with impeccable aim he whipped it at Rage and it collided with his head.

Rage wavered and then turned slowly and closed the distance between them in a few seconds, arms out, causing him to knock Arion straight through an eighteen-wheeler, five blocks away.

"Crap," Arion muttered just before he was hit.

"Found you, punk!" he said once he reached Arion again. People were scattering and screaming at the sight of Rage. Rage picked up the eighteen wheeler and threw it, straight at a crowd of people. Arion ran and intercepted it with his hands, stopping it with only a little bit of skidding and sparks.

"How are you so powerful sometimes, but so weak at others."

"I'll humor you, Titan." Rage cupped his right hand around Arion's throat and threw three punches into his stomach, the last one sending him flying through the brick wall of a building. "I'm runnin' on fear, anger, hate, grief, jealousy, guilt, shame and...well, you get the picture. I'm powered by negativity but fear mostly."

"I'm not scared of you."

"Maybe not, but they are," he said gesturing to the other people, "and I'm feeding off of your anger and hatred towards me and Immortales and the fears within you that I can't see. You're weak. You aren't even close to being a real hero."

Arion clenched his fist and slammed Rage in the chin, sending him flying backwards and very high. "Oh, you should not have done that," he heard from behind him.

He turned to face Huntress. "Bring it on, sweetheart."

"You first," she said, eyes sending off a hint of orange.

He ran at her but she was already in the air, with her foot at his neck.

56.   QUANTUM

Arc and Nexus attacked him. "How's it going Ariel?" Arc called into his communicator. He paused for a couple of seconds. "How *much* longer?"

Lucian flew at him but Arc charged his fist with electricity before punching him right in the face. "Tell your friend that you'll call her back later!" Lucian called from about 20 meters away. He blasted another beam of energy at Arc but a wave of fire flew in front of it, to deflect it. Just as the fire disappeared another Arc of electricity hit Lucian.

"You're not strong enough to fight us," Arc told him.

"Maybe not together." Lucian wrapped a force field around Arc and threw him as hard as he could and he plowed through the trees at the bottom of the cliff.

Nexus looked nervous now, and she stood in a *Mexican stand-off* position, opposite Lucian. She blasted a column of fire and Lucian did a backflip over it, staying in mid-air and blasting her again.

She rolled to the left and threw another blast. Now that he wasn't being simultaneously shocked by electricity, instead of dodging the fire, he stopped it in mid-air in front of him and he sucked it inside of him, absorbing the energy and replenishing his body.

Before Nexus could say anything, Lucian sent a wave of invisible energy which sent her flying back into an enormous boulder, knocking her out, cold.

"What did you do to my *sister!?*" Arc yelled from be-hind Lucian. The arc of electricity was sent flowing directly through his brain. He could *feel* his brain heating up, and he didn't like that feeling *one* bit. He wasn't sure if he was knocked out or dead but everything around him went black.

57.   CIRCE

Jasmine and Meredith continued to follow the glowing man into the forest until they reached a cave. The cave had a huge entrance, 10 meters by 10 meters. Jasmine continued pleading with Meredith but she just wouldn't listen.

Jasmine used a different version of her fire spell to create a ball of fire floating in her hand.

"You really have endless power, don't you?" Meredith asked in awe.

Jasmine shrugged causing the fire to bob up and down. "My dad said that using my powers too much would kill me…"

"Well, he's not the first person that you should trust," Meredith said in a near whisper.

"But everything that has happened to me, involving him has either been to protect me or to...recruit me. Even if he is a murderer, he *is* my dad."

At least you have a dad, Meredith thought and then immediately said, "You heard that, didn't you?"

"Yeah, sorry...sometimes I can't turn this telepathy thing off."

"It's—"

"We are here!" the glowing man said. "I am *Centurion* and this is the legendary Mystica!" He slammed the bottom of his staff on the ground and the whole area was bathed in light. Jasmine quickly extinguished her flame. They twirled around and their eyes were darting to each painting on the walls. "Mystica has been called many things over the years and has been in many different places. You may know it as: *Atlantis, Themyscira, Camelot, El Dorado* and maybe even *Utopia.*"

"All of that...is here?" Meredith asked.

"*Was* here, my dear."

"What happened to them?"

"New rulers, new races...very few of the races still exist

which is why the near-extinct ones are here such as...the
Pegasus or unicorn."

"Why is the dome made of gold?"

"Just a little gift from the parting of El Dorado," he
said with a chuckle. "It gives us fresh air and synthetic sun-
light. It even rains sometimes but only when necessary. Mys-
tica always has a plan...it always seeks out its new rulers and
brings them here out of pure curiosity and when that ruler is
powerful enough...they will take complete control just as
King Arthur did with Camelot and Hippolyta did with The-
myscira. And I believe...that we have found our new queen,"
he said suddenly taking a new interest in Meredith.

58. TITAN

Huntress had taken Arion for a spin sending him flying into multiple things. "Almost there," she said into a communicator before paus-
ing to listen. "JUST A FEW MORE MINUTES, ARC!"

"I don't think so," Arion replied. Huntress lifted her foot to kick
him in the head but the move was easily anticipated by him. He
ducked and swept out her leg from under her causing her to fall on

her back.

"I don't understand how you could ever think that you can live up to what your parents were. You're the son of Atlas, the world's most well-known flier and you can't fly. What does that say? It says you're weak, stupid and *way* out of your league!" Arion had her up against a wall in less than a second. One hand was pushing against her throat and the other was keeping her legs from kicking him.

Just as Arion was about to knock her out all she said was, "Go to hell!" Arion felt something huge and heavy hit him in the head. He fell to the ground, vision blurring. The last thing that he saw was Rage and Huntress towering over him.

"Nighty-night, Titan," Rage said. Then, everything went black.

Arion woke up in a cell, still in his costume. He searched around and saw nothing but darkness around the cage. "Velocity, where am I?"

"Connecting to Global Positioning Satellite right now, Titan."

"As soon as you find out where we are I need you to send coordinates to the team, I don't think I'm getting out of this one alone."

"Right away, sir."

He heard the sound of wings flapping behind him and he turned to see Rage, wings flapping around. "Who are you talking to?" When Arion didn't answer, Rage growled deep in his throat. "I'm just waiting for the go ahead so that I can kill you."

"Waiting for mommy to tell you what to do again?"

"You waiting for your mommy? Oh! Wait, she's dead! I forgot!" Rage barked a laugh.

Arion felt that one deep but hid it as best as he could. "When I get out of here, Rage..."

"I'd like to see you try! I can't even bend those bars at full strength! And you're suspended about 70 feet above the ground. Since you can't fly, I'm hoping that'll be a painful fall. The bars are made out of some African metal that Animon gave us. Apparently he used it against your parents before. It's resistant to nearly anything. Especially brute strength."

"I'm stronger than my parents were and I'm stronger than you are."

"I'll believe it when I see it." He flew away, leaving Arion to his thoughts.

"Titan, the others have been alerted of your location and are on their way, Jasmine has said: Sit tight and we'll be there soon. Will that be all?"

"Yeah, Velocity...that's it."

"Just relax, sir. The team will be here soon."

"I hope so," Arion said sitting down in the center of the cell. "I really hope so."

CHAPTER VIII: RESCUE

59.   QUANTUM

Lucian woke up when Velocity—whoever that was—claimed that Arion was in trouble. Jasmine vouched for him, saying that he was Arion's phone or something like that. "On my way!" he had said. Arc and Nexus were already long gone and Lucian's brain still felt like it had been melted.

Lucian flew across the sky with blinding speed, on his way to the coordinates that were sent to him. He arrived in a few minutes and dropped down in front of an old, abandoned, warehouse.

Jasmine dropped down from the sky so hard that spider-web cracks spread along the concrete. "Where's Meredith?" he asked.

"In the middle of the Atlantic," Jasmine casually replied. "Hyperion?"

Lucian laughed. "You say that like I keep tabs on him!"

"Looks like it's just you and me then," Jasmine said, she stretched out her hand and said, "**Pyrolineum**," causing her hand to set fire, casting an orange light on the inside of the building.

60.   Circe

Jasmine used the same variation of her pyrokinetic spell that she had used in the cave so that they could have some light because the whole place was pitch black. Lucian also lit his hand with glowing red energy. She wasn't too keen on the idea of leaving Meredith at Mystica, but she knew what she was doing and all that Jasmine could think about at that moment was Arion.

She walked in front with Lucian right behind her, shining light on everything that he could. "Titan!?" Jasmine called out. No answer. She could feel through her telekinesis that there was a lot of space around them. They walked down multiple flights of stairs, all the way to the basement.

"Circe! Duck!" Lucian called out. Jasmine saw a pair

of glowing red eyes snap open in front of her. She ducked, and a huge fist missed her by just a hair.

She immediately sent a wave of telekinetic energy out at him, pushing him backwards. Sparks flew as Rage slammed into the electrical panels on the wall.

All of the lights flickered to life to show Rage about 20 feet away, stuck inside the wall and the rest of The Superiors surrounding them slowly.

"Even your own team members bailed on you?" Huntress asked. Jasmine flew at her, arms extended and hit her straight in the gut causing everyone else to attack.

"Where is he, Ariel?" Jasmine asked Huntress while she was pinned. She flipped over and pinned Jasmine instead, slamming her head on the ground repeatedly until she saw spots.

"Do you think that just because we're half-sisters, that somehow makes us friends!? Don't ever call me that again!" Jasmine sent a blast of telekinetic energy towards her sending her straight into the ceiling which is when she saw the cage. She got up and started flying towards it but a huge hand wrapped around her foot and slammed her back into

the ground.

*"**Hydrolineum**," she said causing a spout of water to burst through the ground wrapping around Rage. She used the distraction to fly up to the cage. She saw Arion, sitting in the middle of the cage, looking the other way. "TITAN!" she called. He turned around and looked her right in the eye.*

"Took you guys long enough," he said with a smile but immediately getting serious. "I can't bend the bars...they're too strong."

*"Let's try some heat," she said. "Stand back! **Pyrol**—" she was interrupted by a huge fist slamming her into the side of the cage before she lost consciousness.*

61.   TITAN

Arion watched as Rage slammed Jasmine into the side of the cage. He could *hear* her bones cracking and fracturing. When her body went limp, Rage threw her to the ground but he never expected Arion to get a new ability and Arion saw something in Rage's eyes for the first time...fear.

Arion's eyes began to burn as if he had kept them open for two hours without blinking. His body temperature spiked up to the point that he was sweating like crazy. He saw everything through a yellow-orange glow and then it was *projected*. The heat was so intense that it melted through straight through the bars and hit Rage so hard that it sent him flying through the far wall.

Arion cried out in pain and looked down, burning a hole clean through the floor of the cage, causing him to fall. As he fell the heat coming from his eyes went straight through the ceiling and walls causing everything to collapse around them. His eyes stopped burning and the heat got less and less intense until it was gone altogether.

He scooped Jasmine up and ran out of one of the holes he had made in the side of the building with Lucian hot on his heels.

Once they were outside Arion took Jasmine to Area 02: Health District and was back in a flash. "What were you guys thinking!? Coming in alone like that!?" Arion blurted.

"Hey! Back off!" Lucian warned. "Where were Meredith and Hyperion? Huh?" Arion said nothing. "Next time before questioning the people that were actually here to save you, you should question the people who obviously had better things to do!" Again, Arion said nothing as Lucian flew away.

Arion ran back home to see his dad. Once he had gotten inside and changed his dad questioned him and Arion told him everything. "This beam," his dad asked, "what do you think it was? Pure heat?"

"No...I think it was more than that."

"What triggered it?"

"I was mad and sad and...scared."

"For what reason?"

"Jasmine was being hit, hard...I could hear her bones cracking and breaking. I thought she might die... and Rage said some rude things about mom and I just...let it all out."

"Well...let's see what it is and if you can control it," his dad said with a smile.

"Let's make it quick. I have a meeting tomorrow."

62. <u>QUANTUM</u>

Lucian woke up to his phone ringing. "Lucian, here,"

he answered.

"Where are you? Didn't you get my text?" Jasmine nearly screamed into the phone.

"No, just woke up. You're healed already?"

"Immortality, remember!? We're supposed to be meeting the Prime Minister *in* Ottawa *in* 5 minutes."

"Crap! What time is it?" Lucian asked already out the window and flying to Ottawa.

"2:55 *p.m.!*" He got there less than a minute before the Prime Minister arrived. Prime Minister Strauss was a white guy with short black hair. He walked onto the stage with his wife's hand in one of his and his daughters in the other. She looked about seven. The Prime Minister walked as if he had a limp in both legs, very unsteadily. His wife held a cane for him.

He shook the entire teams' hands and then stood, ready to speak. "Glad you could make it," Lucian muttered to Meredith.

"Likewise," she whispered still smiling for the cameras.

"I know that a lot of people have lost hope ever since the heroes left us all that time ago..." he paused to remember. "But now! The next generation of heroes is upon us!" The crowd around them cheered loudly. Lucian saw Arion's dad in the crowd, nodding instead of clapping. "Here we have our first five:

Titan, *the Teenage Tank*

Circe, *the Enchanting Sorceress*

Quantum, *the Master of Manipulation*

Atlantica, *the Queen of the Ocean* and

Hyperion, *the King of Light.*

Together they form a team that fights not *for* us, but *with* us! Not just for superhumans or humans but for everything. I present to you...The Guardians!" The whole crowd cheered and for one of the few times in his life, he felt appreciated.

"There are only a few people in the world—that our government currently knows about—that possess superhuman abilities," the Prime Minister continued, "If you are in

Canada or anywhere in the world for that matter…find your mask and help. Everyone has the potential to be a hero…only you know when the time is right." The Prime Minister raised his right hand in a wave to the public and everyone cheered.

All of those cheers quickly turned into screams once he heard the boom of a gunshot.

63.   CIRCE

Jasmine and the rest of the team all reacted at the same time. Lucian raised his hands and an energy field went up in-between them but not fast enough to block the bullet. Arion was there in a split second catching the bullet inches from the Prime Minister's face. "Crap!" he yelled. "Hyperion! Get the Prime Minister out of here!" Hyperion flashed in and out of there at least a dozen times in seconds, taking people with him. Jasmine couldn't help but think that she couldn't wait to learn how to teleport.

Jasmine snapped out of her trance and flew up and over the shield that Lucian now put over the civilians so that they would be protected. Arion and Meredith were attempting to calm the public down and explain to them that they were safe as Jasmine flew up to where the bullet came from. She projected her telekinetic energy into a field around her to stop any bullets that may be fired at her. She weaved and bobbed through the air as a secondary precaution.

She saw the broken glass falling from a window and immediately knew where to go. She blasted the wall making a bigger space that she could fly through. She felt a gun barrel pushed against the back of her head as soon as she had touched the floor.

"You're ruining my plans, beautiful," he said in an emphasized Spanish accent.

"You a villain?" She asked, stalling until the rest of The Guardians arrived.

"More like a...vigilante." he said. She could hear the smirk behind his voice. Jasmine attempted to read his mind but all she got was static. "You're not going to get into my head, no matter how hard you try.

"Why are you doing this?"

"I have a friend who can see the future...The Prime

Minister...he's the beginning of the end. I just needed to re-mind him of that. Thank God you were here to save him!" he gushed sarcastically.

"Who are you?" She asked.

"Call me...Blank," he said. The gun barrel dropped from her head and by the time she turned around Blank's black cape was flapping behind his white suit with a black utility belt, black mask with red eyes and a red crosshair on a black circle in the middle of his chest. She tried to stop him with telekinesis, but by then...he was just gone. She looked out the window and he was nowhere to be seen. The rest of the team was there in about a minute. They asked what had happened and all she did was point at a lone sniper rifle in the middle of the floor.

CHAPTER IX: RELAXATION

64.   TITAN

After Jasmine had explained everything tons of questions started to flash in his head. Who is Blank? What did he want? Why try to shoot the Prime Minister? What did he mean when he said that he saw the future?

"Don't worry!" said Lucian slapping him on the back. "It was probably nothing, just an excuse to shoot the Prime Minister." They were gathered in the meeting room of Area 52.

"Good work out there guys..." Arion said. "We've all been working really hard and...I just wanted to reward us...the whole team. See if you can keep up," he said zooming off.

"My dad and I have been working on something on the side that we call...*Project: Guardian*." Arion led them to an industrial area of Toronto. Arion led them into a dark building. "I present to you...*The Central!*" He zoomed off to turn on the lights and what they saw was amazing. There was a giant room with chairs and TV's and computers.

Then there were hallways leading to bedrooms and bathrooms and other things there were at least twenty-five bedrooms.

10 of his dad's sparring drones from the lair walked in. "I took the liberty of uploading Velocity to each and every piece of technology in the building. This used to be the headquarters of The Titans, so just a couple of changes and additions here and there, and...voila."

Jasmine hugged him, tears starting in her eyes. "This is amazing...I've never really had a real home and...I love this."

"No problem!" He let them explore and they each got a Velocity drone to show them around the place. The building was about 5,000 square feet and Arion had seen all of it. His dad and Corbin had let him and Jasmine skip school to meet the Prime Minister so they still have lots of time. Once everyone was settled in, Arion zoomed off to meet Thalia. He changed into civilian clothes and knocked on her door. Thalia lived in a small house near their school.

She swung open the door and saw him standing there. She strode up to him, put her arms around his neck and kissed him for about a minute. "Missed you in class today," she said, her lips an inch from his.

"Went to meet the Prime Minister...no big deal."

"Nothing else?" she asked leading him up to her room by his hand.

"Not really...just saved his life."

"Well that's something," she said. "What happened?"

Once they got to her room, they laid down opposite each other on her bed and Arion told her everything that had happened since his kidnapping and his new power, which he can keep from happening but not fully control, and how he's going to be moving into the house with the team.

Thalia looked disappointed. "Oh, that's cool," she said, forcing a smile.

"What's wrong?" he asked, frowning.

"Nothing...it's just...you're moving in with Jasmine and that bothers me a bit."

"Want me to move in here?" he asked raising his eyebrows.

"That'd be great," she said kissing his lips. "Do you want anything to drink? Water or something?"

"No thanks, not thirsty. Where's your mom?"

"Business, won't be back until tomorrow night."

"Well that gives us plenty of time."

"To do what?"

"Anything you want, sweetie."

"You know I've never been to the Dominican before?"

"Really?" Arion asked, surprised.

"Yeah! I know! My mom said she would take me some day but...never had enough money."

"Well...there's a first time for everything!" He picked her up and zoomed off.

65.   QUANTUM

Lucian was hanging out with Meredith at the new house that Arion had given them. Meredith was half laying on top of him and half in mid-air as he aimlessly floated around his new room. Her head was rested on his chest. "Mer?" he called out.

"Yeah?" she said slightly turning to look in his eyes.

"Why didn't you come to help Arion when he was captured?"

"I found a magical kingdom that I'm destined to rule."

"Say what, now?" Meredith explained everything about
the cave and the islands and the animals. "You're supposed
to be the sole dictator of this place? *Mystica?*"

"Not exactly *sole* ruler," she said, her eyes shimmering
with hope.

Lucian flipped over causing her to fall but he mentally
slowed her fall and laid her down on the bed as he continued to float above her. "I can't be a King! Not yet, anyway..."

"You already call yourself the King of time and...stuff!"

"It's *Master of Manipulation* now but that's different!
It's just a clever codename! Nothing more."

"The Prime Minister called me Queen of the Ocean!"

"Because you're a water manipulator! It's a pretty
basic codename!"

"This conversation is *over*!" she grunted, getting up off

of the bed and storming out of the room. Lucian dropped and landed face first into his pillow and let out loud, long groan.

After a few minutes, he turned over and admired his room. Arion got the walls painted two different shades of red with blue trimming—a lot like his costume—and got at least 100 comic books for him to read and a signed poster by Atlas and all the other Titans from a few years back— which he freaked about for the hour that he had been there. It was hung up just above the TV, which was just a few feet away from the foot of his bed and a computer to the left of the bed. Just to the left of the TV was the door to a private bathroom. On the right was the door to go outside.

"Ugh!" he grunted, admitting to himself that he should go after Meredith.

He got up to go after her and found her in her room, manipulating the water of the indoor pond that Arion had put in front of her bed. The door was already opened but he still knocked as he walked in anyway.

"What?" she asked.

"I'm sorry, okay? I just don't want to be a King, that's it."

"Yeah, that's cool," she said but she sounded disappointed. She created a ball of water about the size of a soccer ball and had two goldfish swimming around in it. "Lucian," she said.

"Yeah?"

"Not you," she turned around and smiled at him as the water-ball lowered itself back into the pond. "The fish asked what your name was."

"Is it weird being able to talk to fish and stuff?" he asked sitting on the floor beside her, in front of the pond.

"Not really, it's cool. Remember the day you asked me out? The day you disappeared?" Lucian had forgotten all about his dad and his deadline until that moment.

"Yeah," he said, uneasily. "What about it?"

"For the first time ever...I really felt a connection with that shark, the one that got his nose broken by Arion. I've visited him a few times and we just have a bond. He said that he was orphaned when he was young, his parents and younger sister were hunted and captured by humans illegally. His parents managed to hide him though. I healed him and ever since then...we've been inseparable."

"Like a pet?"

"More than that...like a friend."

"My girlfriend is friends with a fish. Great! Don't leave me for him, you know!"

She playfully punched him in the arm. "You know I wouldn't do that," she said, kissing him softly.

"I hope not. I don't think he can do this," he said. He raised his hand and her clothes started to disappear starting at her shoes.

"Lucian, stop," she said laughing.

"Are you sure?" he asked. Her knees were showing now.

"Lucian," she warned. Her thighs started to show and it was getting higher. A blast of water erupted from the pond sending Lucian sliding along the hardwood floor. Within a second he was completely dry and all of the water was back in the pond. Meredith's pants were now *extremely* short-shorts.

"Not fair!" Lucian called in-between a coughing fit.

"Life isn't fair, *Quantum.*" She kissed him on the cheek and walked out of the room. When he didn't follow she popped her head back in. "Are you coming or what?"

"I don't know! Am I going to be blasted with water!?"

"Depends! Are you going to try taking my clothes off, again?"

"If I wanted them off, they'd be off!"

"Whatever!"

"You aren't going to change?" he asked as he started to follow her.

"Nah. I think I might *keep* these for a while." As soon as she turned the corner Lucian internally yelled, *YES!*

66.   CIRCE

Jasmine and Meredith had been back and forth between their house and the new H.Q. Her room was set up almost the same as everyone else's except it was bigger. She had an extra half of a normal room and a double sized bathroom.

"Favouritism is nice sometimes," she muttered to herself. She had a desk with a laptop on it and a bookshelf built around it with all of her favourite books, magazines and even her mom's sorcery book to the right of her bed. The door to leave was directly in front of her bed and the bathroom was on the left wall.

Jasmine nearly bumped into Hyperion when she walked out of her door. "Sorry!" they both said at the same time causing a smile to form on Jasmines face.

"What are you doing?" she asked as she moved to his side.

"Walking," he replied. "You?"

"Also walking." There was a moment of awkward silence until Jasmine finally said, "Do you want to go somewhere? Right now? Anywhere really...just to get away?" He looked at her with eyes that showed no difference from his skin. He walked for a minute, thinking it over while Jasmine

was internally beating herself up for asking him that even though she *knew* that he liked Meredith.

"Yeah, Jasmine. Sure," she followed him outside and he asked her where she wanted to go.

"Anywhere."

Let's see Arion do this! Jasmine overheard in his head. He picked her up in his arms and flew up as high as he could at the speed of light and then shifted directions heading north-east.

They arrived in Paris in less than a second. Hyperion created a small platform, fit for two people on the tip of the Eifel Tower, their legs hanging off the side. "I have a feeling that you want to talk."

"I don't think you'd want to hear it," Jasmine replied with a forced smile.

"Lay it on me, doll," he said.

She just blurted it all at once. "It's Arion...I'm not sure whether he likes me or Thalia and if he likes me, why is he dating her. Because he acts like he likes me around me, but when we're both there he acts like he likes her."

"In my opinion," Hyperion started, "Arion is a flirtatious, unfaithful guy who's bound to hurt any girl that comes into his life."

"Not if she's immortal," Jasmine murmured.

"Huh?" he asked.

"Nothing," she quickly replied.

"If you ask me, doll...you deserve a lot better."

"Thanks," she replied. "I just don't...know what to do."

"We should start by stopping that plane from crashing into us," Hyperion said, pointing up.

"Do we EVER get a break?" she cried.

"Evil never sleeps, doll," he said, raising off of the platform, "never."

Once Hyperion was close enough he created a slide out of energy to try and bring the plane to a less populated area but his construct wasn't strong enough. "Hyperion!" Jasmine yelled over the crackle of flames and roar of the engine. He turned to look at her. "Get the passengers out! I can handle the plane!"

Hyperion nodded, "Sure thing, doll," he said and tele-ported into the plane. Jasmine went under the plane and used her telekinesis to augment her strength and create a field around the plane. She pushed up as hard as she could until the plane was climbing upwards on an angle, just narrowly missing the tower. Jasmine started to sweat from using her powers too much. Hyperion flashed in front of her.

She tilted the plane so that it would still climb if she let go. She turned to Hyperion. "Everyone off?"

"Yeah, what should we do with it?"

"We're going to blow it up," she said, putting on her devious smirk. "Put a ball around me and the plane as big as you can with one hole and it has to be bigger than me, got it?"

"I got it," he said. He raised his hand to the plane that had begun to descend and created a barrier around it. Jasmine flew through the hole that was placed for her. She found the gas tank which was on the opposite side of the fire.

"**Pyrolineum**!" she said aiming directly for the gas tank. As soon as it ignited she flew out of the barrier as fast as she could. "Close it!" she yelled as soon as she got out.

She spun around in the air creating a telekinetic field around it and the plane exploded within the barrier. The barrier contained the fire until cracks started to spread all over it. The ball exploded right in front of her and Hyperion sending them flying backwards through the air.

67.   <u>TITAN</u>

Arion and Thalia were lying down on the nice white sand of the beach in Punta Cana, Dominican Republic. They were both wearing swimsuits so Thalia's head was resting against Arion's bare chest.

She looked him right in the eyes, and said, "I love you." Arion was so shocked by what she said he was speechless. "Sorry...I just had to say it—" Arion stopped her by firmly planting his lips against hers.

"Thalia, I fell in love with you from the minute I laid my eyes on you in the first grade. I love everything about you and you know that I'd do absolutely anything for you."

"Is that why you brought me here?"

"Actually, it was to see you in a bathing suit," he said with a smirk.

She playfully punched him in the stomach, "Shut up!" she said, but couldn't help but smile too. "You could look through my clothes at any time you wanted!"

"But! I haven't, because I love and respect you...as far as you know." She rolled her eyes and kissed him on the cheek. "Want something to drink?" he asked.

"Piña Colada would be great, thanks."

"Back in a flash," he zoomed away to the nearest hotel.

"**Arion**," came a voice through his communicator.

"What's up Velocity?" he asked carrying the drinks in his hand.

"**There is a fire three blocks from your current positioning. I wasn't sure whether you were on the job or not.**"

"I'm always on the job," he said. He mentally told his costume-shifter to activate as he zoomed back to Thalia. Just as he handed her both drinks his suit flashed on. "Sorry, beautiful. There's a fire just up the street."

"Yeah, yeah," she said waving her hand. "Duty calls!"

"I love you so much," he said zooming off.

"I love you too," he heard in a whisper with his super hearing. The fire was nothing big so all he had to do was run around a few times to extinguish the flames.

He was back at the beach with Thalia in seconds. "Hey there, beautiful," he said from behind her. "You out here all alone?"

"Nah, my boyfriend is just around the corner and he'll be here in a few minutes."

"That gives us plenty of time," he said. His costume switched back into his swim shorts.

"So...do you want to go for a swim?"

"You know it, baby," she said, putting her arms around his neck and kissing him. She got an evil look in her eye. "How far do you think you could throw me?" she asked.

"Back to your house if I really tried and wanted to burn you to a crisp."

"How about just...a few meters into the ocean."

"I don't know..." Arion began to think.

"Pllleeeaaassseee!" she begged. "I'll love you forever!"

"Well in that case..." he paused to listen to his communicator.

"Hyperion and Jasmine aren't answering our transmissions!" Lucian yelled. "You're our second fastest, we last saw them in Paris, few away of the Eifel tower.

"I can't get a bird's eye view!" Arion said, earning an odd look from Thalia.

"That's what Meredith and I are doing! Just get here, quick!"

Before Arion could say anything to Thalia she kissed him on the lips. "Go ahead," she said. "Make your girlfriend proud."

"Want me to take you home?"

"Is it on your way?"

"Everything's on my way," he said, "and no mission is more important than you."

Thalia leapt into his arms. "Then carry me into the sunset," she said.

"If you insist," he said, darting off across the ocean.

68.   QUANTUM

Lucian flew above the Eifel tower waiting for Meredith

to meet back up with him. She floated in on one of her so-lidified clouds and shook her head. "This can't be happen-ing."

"What if they just got hitched or something?" Lucian suggested.

"I doubt they'd get married at 15 and 16," they heard over their communicator. "Just seeing you guys up there makes me nauseas! Get down here so we can make a plan."

"On our way, Titan."

Once they got down to the bottom of the tower, Arion demanded to know what they knew. "There was an out of control plane, they got everyone out and then literally de-stroyed every last bit of the plane but the explosion sent them flying. We've heard that from a few people."

Arion looked up and pointed, "That's where the plane blew up," he said. "There are four trails of heat going in four different directions...looks like some debris survived the explosion after all."

"How do you know?"

"New advancement of my X-Ray vision, I guess, infra-red vision? Try to look into it, see if you can. If so, you and Meredith follow two and I'll follow two, we'll see where we end up."

"I can see it, faintly but I got it. Follow it before the trail goes cold, no pun intended." Arion zoomed off in one direction and Meredith followed Lucian to another.

They got to the first one and all they found was a flaming plane engine. Meredith doused the flames and Lucian absorbed the atoms so that nobody would have to clean it up later.

They retraced their steps and went back to the site of the explosion and followed a different trail this time. Once they reached the end, all they saw was a glowing body, glowing dimmer than they were used to. There was smoke billowing up from where he had landed in the next city over. Meredith propped up his head on her lap as Lucian tried to diagnose the problem.

"Let's take him to Area 02, they can probably help

him." Meredith nodded as Lucian created a platform to prop them both up on. He may not like Hyperion and Hyperion may not like him but, someone in need was someone in need, no matter what. He flew them to Area 02 as fast as he could.

"I found Jasmine," Arion called into the communicators.

"I'll stay with Hyperion," she said giving Lucian a quick kiss. "Go ahead." Lucian nodded and flew to Arion's coordinates.

69.   <u>CIRCE</u>

Jasmine stood in a forest. The last thing she remembered was being blown away by that exploding plane. Her dad appeared in front of her in a flash of purple light. "What do you want?" she demanded.

"Nothing, just wanted to see my daughter! Is that a crime?" he asked, spreading his hands in a questioning gesture. The cynical, sadistic smile that he flashed at the end

didn't show love though.

"It is if you're a criminal and were told to stay away from her!" she retorted.

"I just want to talk, Jasmine."

"Then talk, I guess I don't have a choice but to listen."

He nodded grimly. "I'm only here to advise you about your powers. Soon you'll be able to do this, enter the dreams of people, and manipulate their minds."

"I won't! That's not what heroes do!"

"You think of yourself as a hero?" He asked. He laughed so loud that her dream turned fuzzy. "You're no hero! You're a pawn in something much bigger than yourself or your stupid little superhero squad. There are much greater forces at work right now Jasmine, much bigger than me or you or that little do-gooder that you are in love with!" Jasmine felt her face getting red. "Wake now, child. Your love awaits you!" His laugh began to fade as she was pulled out of her dream.

Jasmine awoke to a violent shake. When her eyes opened she saw Arion sitting beside her with her back on his lap. "What happened?" she asked getting up.

"Plane, explosion, Paris...anything ringing a bell?"

"Yeah...I remember. Where's Hyperion!?"

"He's okay...for now. He's at Area 02 with Meredith."

As if on cue, Lucian touched down beside them. "What is it?"

"I never told you guys this," Jasmine started, "but I'm really glad that we found each other. I feel like it was fate, for me to be in the store across the street, Lucian who just happened to be flying over us and Arion just happening to be watching the news."

"I really don't think we could've gotten a better team," Lucian agreed.

There was a silent agreement between them and they flew off, leaving Arion to run back home.

70. <u>TITAN</u>

Once Arion got home, his dad took him straight to their under-ground lair. His dad set up three different targets after Arion changed into his regular clothes. One of them was circling the room at 100 miles per hour and the other two were stand-stills.

"Just concentrate on what activates it," his dad said, referring to his *Laser Vision*. "All the anger that you have inside, just let it all out. But! Don't burn anything except the targets. Put these in," his dad handed him two clear contacts. "These will see what it's made out of."

"Okay, I got this," Arion told himself. *Think about how mad you were when Rage showed up and how sad you were when mom died,* he thought to himself. Neither of the two worked. An idea popped into his head. He pictured Jasmine getting beaten and almost just as instantly an intense beam of heat erupted from his eyes and burned everything that he looked at. Thankfully his dad had left the room quickly. Seeing her *hurt* is what activated it.

"At least you can turn it on," his dad said through the microphone on the other side of the scorched glass. "Turning it off is the problem..."

Arion tried again and again but nothing. "Try getting happier," his dad said. "What was the happiest moment in your entire life?"

Jasmine! He said to himself. He looked directly at the first target and he burned a hole through it. He thought about the day that his dad had first told him that he was a super powered alien. It caused the beam to stop, abruptly.

He continued like this until he finally had it under control. When he walked out of the room he saw his dad holding a hologram in his hand. It was two eyeballs, one in each hand. "Its solar beams," his dad said.

"Huh?" Arion asked.

"Your eyes are redirecting the solar energy that you absorb," his dad replied. "This is amazing. You're getting so many powers... more than your mother or me. You really are a spectacular kid, you know that?"

"So I've been told," he muttered. "Thanks, dad."

"No problem." His dad put his arm around his shoulder and walked out of the room, "So...Dominican Republic, huh?"

"Were you spying on me!?" Arion demanded.

"No, I heard about the fire that you put out. Good work."

"Thanks."

"You really need to get a new look. People trust you better when they can see your face. The hood doesn't help."

"It doesn't?"

"Not always. I think you've established your two identities...maybe it's time to show your face. A power that I used to have
was a very limited version of DNA Manipulation, but only in my face. I
could make my skin a little bit darker or lighter, change my eye colour or hair colour and I could manipulate the shape of my nose or
mouth ever so slightly and I could grow or...un-grow hair at will.

"Try changing... your hair colour, that's the easiest. Just pick a
colour and concentrate on that colour as hard as you can." Arion focused on a colour (or shade), white. He concentrated as hard as he
could and when he reopened his eyes and looked in the mirror, he
had a patch of white by his sideburns. "Now, take it away."

Arion focused but instead heard something. "Leave me alone!" he
heard Thalia scream, followed by her footsteps and heavier ones behind
her.

"Thalia!" he exclaimed and blurred off.

When he arrived to her neighbourhood he realized that they had
her pinned up against a wall just down the street. "Titan," he heard
through his communicator. "Something was stolen, extremely valuable.

We need to get to *Cooze Natural Sciences*, now."

Arion turned off the communicator and stepped in-between Thalia and the three thugs. "I'm going to need you guys to leave my girl-friend alone. Can you do that?" The first guy swung at him and he grabbed his arm, spun around and threw him into a wall. "I warned you."

Both of the other guys sprinted at him both throwing random punches and kicks but Arion dodged every single one of them. He slammed his hand into one of their chests and he flew back ten feet. Arion could tell that his ribs were cracked. The last guy pulled out a small sub-machine gun and fired at him. All of the bullets bounced off of him, two of them ricocheting back into the guy who was firing. "Velocity, notify the police, please. And a couple ambulances"

"As you wish, Arion."

He turned to look at Thalia. "All good?"

She nodded and he took her to The Central.

71.   QUANTUM

"TITAN! ARION!" he called into the communicator. He

shook his head, "he turned it off! That son of a—"

"Doesn't matter," Jasmine said, "You, Meredith and I can handle this one." They flew to Cooze Natural Sciences in California to investigate what was stolen. The first things that they saw once they got there were the flashing lights from the emergency vehicles and the smoke rising into the sky. Once they landed they saw the huge hole in the wall which they knew could only be caused by one person.

Rage, Jasmine said to them telepathically.

They walked into the building. "This is a restricted area!" a police officer said attempting to stand in their way. "There's no way I'm letting a bunch of kids into a facility like this." Jasmine raised her hand and he lifted into the air above them and they walked under him. After they had passed, Jasmine lowered him.

Lucian saw the holes in the walls leading to one room. When they walked inside there was a man talking to some officers. He had a short, pointed, white beard that went all the way up the sides of his face and a mop of curly white hair. Once he saw the kids he excused himself from the police and went to talk to them.

"*Circe, Atlantica, Quantum,*" he said as if greeting them.

"And you are...?" Lucian asked.

"Professor Valentine," he said. "I aided in the creation of the machine that was stolen."

"Well Professor," Jasmine began, "can you tell us what happened here?"

"I don't know how they knew it was here. There were three of them, big guy, light gray and a black girl, she was fast and another girl who could change her size."

"*Rage, Huntress and Pixie,*" Meredith stated as if it wasn't obvious. Lucian gave her a sarcastic, *you don't say* look.

"They attacked me, I wasn't badly wounded and thankfully I was the only worker in the lab. They took the machine and ran. When I woke up the police were shining flashlights in my eyes."

"Professor Valentine...I need to know *exactly* what this machine can do."

"It's nearly impossible to use it without the right brains and technology," Valentine continued.

"They have two extremely smart twins on their team...they might be able to crack it," Jasmine retaliated.

"It would need a near endless power source to function properly. Something that wouldn't need to recharge. 60% of people have the potential."

"Professor!" Lucian called. "We need to know! What. Does. The. Machine. Do?"

The professor looked each of them directly in the eyes, Lucian last. "It enhances the Evolutionary Gene inside a person's body. If the radius is large enough, it could be 60% of the world's population."

"What's the Evolutionary Gene?" Lucian demanded.

"It's...it's the gene that is inside Evolutionaries—people with powers. This device will activate the dormant part of their DNA and bestow abilities on these people. If all of these people have the potential..."

"Some might be good," Meredith said.

"And others might be evil," Lucian concluded. "*Extremely* evil."

72. Circe

"WHY WOULD YOU MAKE SOMETHING LIKE THAT!?" Jasmine screamed at him, lifting him off of the ground with telekinesis.

"I was under the Prime Minister's orders!" he choked out. Jasmine dropped him on the ground with a thud. "The Prime Minister and I went to the University of Toronto together," he began. "We became good friends but if I would ever go to his dorm, there'd be posters everywhere of superheroes. We both majored in biology so we began working on a serum...one that could give humans powers.

"We tried so many times until once, he grew impatient enough to test it on himself," he continued. "I told him—begged him—not to! He did it anyways. He gained super

speed, super jumping and super strength in his legs. The serum wore out and destroyed his legs from the inside out."

"Is that why he walks with a limp?" Lucian asked. Jasmine thought back because she hadn't even thought twice about the limp until now.

Professor Valentine nodded. "This is why he hired me, to see if I could activate the superhuman genes that give normal people special abilities. If it gave him his speed back..."

"It might be able to heal him," Meredith finished for him.

"Precisely," the Professor agreed.

"We'll do our best to get it back," Lucian said.

"And I will be here, trying to help you in whatever way I can. One more thing before you guys go...the machine is unstable and hasn't been tested yet. It could...kill everyone who doesn't have the potential for powers. Rage as you call him, interrogated me and asked me how long until it would be in working order. I told him about a week or so."

"Dr. Valentine..." Meredith began, "next time, just tell us all of the information first because that was...kind of important."

"My apologies," he said. A blur and whoosh zoomed in and stopped beside them. Arion was standing there watching them.

"What's up?" he asked.

"Doctor," Lucian said, "could you excuse us for a second. We need a little team meeting." The doctor nodded and strode away to go see the police officers. Arion turned and watched the doctor leave. When he turned back, Lucian's fist was flying for his face. It hit him hard enough to cause a shockwave and to send him stumbling back a few feet.

Arion closed the distance between himself and Lucian in nanoseconds. "You really want to do this now, Quantum?" his eyes started glowing orange and Jasmine felt the need to step in.

*Just as Lucian was about to hit Arion again Jasmine called, "**Chriona Mrionte**," with her hand aimed at Arion and Meredith shot ice cold water from the sprinkler system into Lucian's face.*

"Stop it!" Meredith whispered.

The officers and the professor turned to look at them.

*"Everything is alright!" Jasmine called. "Just a slight **misunderstanding**." Her voice echoed throughout the room in a sweet, sugary tone.*

The policemen continued to question the doctor with a slightly mystified look in their eyes. "Yeah, just a misunderstanding," Meredith and Lucian agreed with the same look in their eyes.

"What the hell was that?" Arion asked her. "I heard the same ringing as whenever you try to read my mind."

"My dad told me that my powers were strong." Jasmine said. "Telepathy is controlling and manipulating everything inside the mind. Maybe...maybe..."

"What?" Arion urged her.

"Maybe I just controlled their minds."

73. <u>TITAN</u>

"Maybe we should keep it a secret, just for now," Arion suggested once they were back at the base.

"I think you're right," Jasmine agreed. She followed him down the hall up to her room.

"Night, Jaz," he said.

"Well I was going to invite you in, maybe fill you in on the mission or something..."

"Actually, I have a couple of other things to do."

Jasmine sighed. "'Course," she said.

"Sorry, maybe tomorrow." He winked at her and then walked into his own room across the hall.

"Fill you in on the mission?" Thalia scoffed.

"She was just trying to be nice!" Arion replied, sounding skeptical himself. He laid down on the bed beside her. "When's your mom coming back, again?"

"Tomorrow evening."

"Well where are you sleeping tonight?"

"Don't really want to go back..."

"Velocity, get a guest room ready please," he said standing up.

"Not really what I meant," she muttered.

"You're not staying in here," Arion sternly said.

"Why not?" she pleaded. As Arion thought about an answer he looked around his room. His walls were a mix of blue, red and white.

His bed was in the far, left corner with the TV in front of it, beside the door. His TV doubled as a computer and he had a bathroom door to the right of his bed.

"You know exactly why not," he said.

"Enlighten me," she said, crossing her arms. Arion couldn't help but smile at her green eyes and at her mouth that was turned into a pouty frown.

"Um, try we're both fifteen and you shouldn't even be here in the first place."

"That is NOT fair!" she nearly screamed.

"Some people in this building are trying to sleep." She snorted, flipped her hair and walked out. "Women," he muttered to himself.

"What?" she called back.

"Nothing!" he said as he followed her out, shaking his head.

CHAPTER X: STOLEN

74.   QUANTUM

Lucian tried to tune out whatever Arion and Thalia were saying and get some sleep but the same image flashed in his head from a couple nights before. It showed three silhouettes. They began to glow and then they morphed into Arion, himself and Jasmine all in full hero costumes, just a little bit older. "He has been summoned!" they all chanted at once.

His eyes snapped open and it was already morning. He got up and smelled something delicious. By the time he got dressed and went into the kitchen, the rest of the team was already there. Thalia was wearing one of Arion's t-shirts—Lucian knew because it was too long—and her own pair of shorts which earned a deepened scowl from Jasmine.

Jasmine turned her head and looked at him and he raised his hand as if to say *Cool it.* She sighed.

In a few minutes Velocity had used one of his robots to serve up bacon, eggs, toast, sausage and a bunch of other great food. He even had multiple types of beverages prepared for Meredith. Just as everyone was about to start eating, Hyperion stood and teleported out of sight.

Everyone was silent for a few seconds but then realized how hungry they were and started to dig in.

After they were finished and laughing and talking an alarm began to blare, bathing the room in red light.

Arion zoomed out with Thalia and then returned solo. He placed his hand on the table and a holographic screen shot up from the center. On one of the screens was showing live footage of a police chase in San Diego. "No big deal," Lucian stated, crossing his arms.

As soon as he said it, one of the police cars lifted into the air and was sent flying into a building across the street. Another car lifted up and flew straight at the helicopter that was filming, causing the screen to change to white noise.

"Suit up," Arion said touching his belt. Arion was the first one to San Diego with Hyperion, who amazingly heard the alert too. Lucian got there pretty quickly too, carrying Meredith.

There were three cars and twice as many police cars. Every couple of seconds the police cars would randomly roll over or smash into each other.

Just as Lucian was about to create a force field in front of the cars, Arion sped past and stood in front of the lead car. Walking towards it slowly. Just as the car came up to him, he reacted at supersonic speed, kicking both front tires halfway across the street and then, he pounded both fists on the hood, causing the car to flip over him. As another car passed by, he punched the rear left side and it spun out of control.

An unseen force then took him and threw him straight up into the air, thousands of feet above them. That is when Lucian snapped into action. "JAZ!" he called. She looked at him and he pointed to the sky. She immediately understood and took off after Arion.

Lucian went back to his first plan of putting the force field in front of them and when he did all of the cars passed directly through it, except for the unlucky cop cars.

Lucian kept the fact that he was stunned to himself and flew after the cars. A wall of water erupted from the road a few hundred feet ahead and Meredith was standing on top of it. Once the cars were close enough, they pulled together into a line and a hole big enough for one car to fit through emerged in the water-wall and each car followed closely behind the last.

Jasmine flew down with Arion in her arms and she put him down in front of the cars. "That. Is. IT!" he used his solar vision—or whatever he called it—to such an intense temperature that it melted the pavement. It started to bubble and boil. The cars began to stick to the pavement with their tires sizzling too.

The police opened the car doors but there was nobody inside of them. Arion took off very angrily and Jasmine sped after him.

75.   CIRCE

"Just CHILL!" she yelled over the roar of Arion break-ing the sound barrier. He stopped abruptly causing her to smack into him.

"What?" he hissed.

"I should be asking you that!" she cried. "What's your problem?"

"I can't freaking fly, that's my problem!"

"So what?"

"I'm the leader of this team and I can't even master the most basic ability known to all superheroes! You—no of-fense—had to catch me and bring me down safely because I am afraid of heights."

"No you aren't," she yelled.

"What are you talking about?" he demanded.

"You aren't. You got over that fear a while ago!" Arion said nothing. He straightened his jaw and waited for her to continue. "You can't fly because you don't want to! You can't fly because your mom couldn't. You didn't say one

word or scream or even close your eyes while we were coming back down. There is something *seriously* blocking your
ability to fly consciously. It's like you're...mentally *honouring* your mom by *not flying.*"

Before he could say anything, she grabbed his hand and
extended her telekinetic field to him. She lifted him up into
the air and flew over San Diego with him. "If you ask me, it
seems like you enjoy being up here!" she yelled over the
wind. She could've sworn that she saw the hint of a smile on
his lips.

She created a duplicate of her hand out of invisible telekinetic energy and slid it into place where her hand was. She
removed her telekinetic field from him and he didn't even notice. He continued to fly with her imaginary hand in his and
she drifted further and further away. Arion began to lift further up. "I feel like I'm controlling my own movements, Jaz."

"That's because you are," she said from a few meters
behind him.

"What the—" he didn't even get to finish before he
plummeted a few hundred meters. Jasmine flew after him and
pulled him back up. By this time they were just a few minutes

away from their The Central in Brampton. She lowered herself and landed them both.

"You know that school starts in four minutes, right?"
she asked.

"Dammit," he said, pushing the button on his belt.

As soon as they were ready, Arion super sped them to
school. "That was…fast…" she said once they arrived to
school.

"Now you know how I feel all the time. It's fun, huh?"
she nodded and followed him into class.

Mr. Shuster walked in a few minutes later. After ten
minutes of trying to tell them the differences between latitude
and longitude Arion sent Jasmine a message. Go to the wash-
room, Jaz. Now.

She didn't ask any questions. She asked Mr. Shuster and
he allowed it. 5 minutes later Arion met her in the hallway in
front of the girl's bathroom. He grabbed her hand and super
sped her out. "Now, Velocity!" he called out.

Jasmine heard the alarms going off in the school recit-
ing: "Initiate Lockdown Procedure! THIS IS A LOCK

DOWN! THIS IS NOT A DRILL!" With police and nuclear-like sirens in the background.

She turned to him and gasped. *"You didn't!"*

"Oh but I did," he said. He tapped his belt and told her to follow him.

"What's this about?" she asked once they had gotten to wherever he wanted them to go. They were in the middle of an abandoned section of town on the street.

"Velocity sent me a message about a group of villains gathering at these coordinates. Think we should call the team?"

*"Nah! **Phantumus Exponesis**!"* she yelled, grabbing his hand. *"I think we can handle this one on our own."*

"Why are we going ghost?" he asked.

"Obviously if they aren't in the sky or on the ground they're…"

"Underground. You're a genius."

*"**Yeah, I know**,"* she said in a random language.

"Was that French?" Arion asked.

"Maybe. Don't let go of my hand, at all, okay?"

"Don't have to tell me twice," he said. If they weren't invisible he would've seen her face turn as red as an apple.

They hovered down through the street. "They can't see or feel us but they can definitely hear us so be very, extremely quiet!" she harshly whispered.

"Got it."

After a few seconds they descended through the ceiling of a huge clearing, a place where people used to gather to do illegal things or have illegal party's hundreds of years ago.

There was a stage up against the front wall with one man standing on it with about a dozen items draped with sheets. The man was wearing a full body suit that was blood red with white polka dots all over him. The Dot, she thought to herself once she recognized him. In front of the stage was at least two dozen lesser-known villains like Sneezo—with the ability to make others sneeze,—Marxin and others.

"Here," The Dot began, pulling the sheet off of one of the cases, "is a state of the art particle stabilizer! It'll rip anything apart, molecule by molecule or stabilize most unstable devices...do I hear 10,000?"

"15!" called Marxin.

"20!"

"50!"

"100!"

"100,000 dollars! Going once? Going twice? SOLD! To the woman in green!"

Jasmine noticed Arion's hand get tighter around hers. She looked at him but he wasn't there—that was good, but she knew what was coming. It was a simple: Achoo, but everyone below was blown away.

76. <u>TITAN</u>

Arion sneezed and a brand new super power was activated. He blew every single one of them halfway across the giant room. During the sneeze he accidentally let go of Jasmines hand and fell hard on one of the tables. "Super Breath..." he said, "not bad."

He turned and raised his arm just in time to block Marxin's fist. The force sent Arion flying back into one of the walls.

The ground began to shake and water shot from the ground aimed at him. He activated his solar vision and retaliated against the water. The water evaporated causing a thin layer of steam to surround them. He heard a sharp clap and he flew across the room smashing straight into another wall. When he reopened his eyes there were at least a dozen guys standing around him, all the steam, gone.

"HIS DAD PUT ME BEHIND BARS!" one yelled. Everyone else started to yell in agreement. Arion activated his speed and time slowed around him. He jumped straight at Marxin, presumably the most powerful person there, and knocked him out with one swift kick to his head. During the kick he also knocked a guy with giant hands and feet—same one who clapped and sent him flying to the other side of the room—with his hand.

"2 down," he muttered, "22 or so left to go." He tried to take out the hardest ones first using a combination of his powers and he caught glimpses of Jasmine holding her own.

Just as Arion broke into a run someone yelled, "STOP!" and everything froze, including Arion. Only his eyes could move. He saw The Dot walking around as if checking everyone out. Arion slowly gained feeling back in his body until he was normal again. He tried using his speed but it wouldn't work. He looked up and saw Jasmine locked in combat with two other flyers except they weren't moving, just hovering in mid-air.

"What did you do!?" Arion called out to The Dot. The Dot turned as if he didn't know that he had even been able to move.

"How did you do that?" he demanded.

"Do what?"

"Stop time! Only two people in the entire world were fast enough to do that, Mercury and Marvella."

"How did I do it?" he asked himself.

"You must've been super speeding when I said it...take your friend and go!"

"Why are you letting me go?"

"Your mother showed me the wrong in my ways once...she was good to me. But... once you try evil, you just...can't stop. I'm sorry about her death, although I may be 10 or so years too late."

Arion nodded and super leaped into the air, pulling Jasmine down with him. The Dot looked at his fingernails as if he were bored, even though they were covered by his costume. "9...8...7," Arion held the frozen body of Jasmine and found the staircase, zooming out of the underground room. When they reached the surface, time resumed and Jasmine punched him straight in the face.

"OW!" he cried out, clutching his nose.

Jasmine leaped out of his arms and said, "How? What? Who?"

"I'll explain later," he said rubbing his nose. "We've got to go! Now!"

They got back to their Headquarters and Arion explained everything to her about The Dot and his mom and absolutely everything. "So that's why he just...let us go?"

Arion nodded. He was sitting at the kitchen counter beside Jasmine, sipping a magical—no pun intended—cup of hot chocolate that she had made. There was a whoosh of air beside him and the solid gold decorative writing on the wall that had each of their hero names, disappeared. Arion immediately entered super speed mode and he saw a guy, no older than 16, taking all of their stuff. He was walking in speedster-time but to everyone else, they were blurs and whooshes.

"HEY!" Arion called. The kid looked at him. He was wearing a pair of sport goggles so Arion could see his lime green eyes behind them. He had short black hair styled upwards, white skin, but tanned as if he had been under the sun for a while, and he was wearing a green t-shirt with black jeans.

"Whoa!" he said. "The famous, Titan! I finally found you. I've been in every single room of just about every building in the city. I just *knew* that you guys had to be in one of em'!" He tossed the bag of stuff that he was taking to the floor.

"What do you want?" Titan growled.

"What do you think I want!? A race!" he zoomed off and Arion chased after him.

"I'm the fastest kid alive!" Arion called to him. "My mom was the fastest superhero!"

The kid sped up once he reached the water and turned around, running backwards. Arion usually just had a blur of colour from his clothes behind him whenever he super sped, but this guy was the real deal. He had that with green and yellow electricity coursing through that blur. "Actually, second fastest. First was my dad."

Arion's eyes widened. "You're Mercury's kid?" he demanded.

"BINGO!" Arion sped up. He needed to catch this kid, ask him some questions. "You have a natural…enhanced speed," he continued. "My dad was an entity of speed, given his powers of speed by the God Hermes, himself. Named himself after his roman side. Guess it was hereditary."

"Where have you been all this time?" Arion asked, following the kid jumping over a cruise ship except this guy did it all backwards. "How did you jump that high?"

"Gather up enough speed and you get that extra push. I've been around. Don't know where my dad is…or my mom."

"What's your name?"

"Name's Maximus Sparks. I would tell you to call me Max but, I don't know you like that." Max broke the sound barrier and continued to run. Arion followed closely until the sonic boom rang his ears too. "'Till next time, Arion. Call me if you need anything." He winked and then turned to face the front again.

"How do you know that name?" he demanded but Max was already gone. All Arion could see was a small explosion of green electricity and light as Max got where Arion never could. He ran faster than light itself.

77.   QUANTUM

Lucian walked into the room just in time to see Arion zoom out. Jasmine sat there stunned until Lucian cleared his throat behind her.

"What happened to him?" Lucian asked.

"We were in the middle of talking and then he was just...gone." Jasmine looked at the floor, disappointed.

"Maybe it was a hero thing?" Lucian suggested trying to get her hopes up.

"He probably would've told me or brought me with him—" Another blur of blue entered the room and Arion was sitting in his chair at the counter again, breathing heavily.

He got up, went to the fridge and pulled out four water bottles. He chugged them all at super speed. "Sorry Jaz," he said. He explained everything about the speedster, how he was faster than the speed of light and how he is Mercury's son. Arion got up and looked for something. "Are you kidding me!? In the time it took me to get back here, 3 seconds—give or take a few—he came back took the bag of stuff he was going to steal and more and left before I even got back!" He felt around his pockets, "*and* he took my wallet!"

"He was given the power by the Roman God, Mercury, right?" Lucian asked.

"Hermes, actually."

"God of speed, thievery and trickery. This...*Max* guy travelled across the world at blinding *speed*, *stole* tons of stuff and *tricked* you into leaving The Central undefended from *Attack by Speedster*."

"This kid is a pro!" Jasmine said. "We've got to catch him, turn him in."

"We'll tell Hyperion to keep a lookout but that's the best that we can do, none of us can see something moving at the speed of light except light itself." Arion said, his blue eyes daring them to challenge him. He looked hurt, as if his pride had taken a punch in the face.

"Good thing, we do have something's to go on," Arion continued. "He steals, look for unsolved thefts around the world that could relate to him, his name is Maximus "Max" Sparks and his dad is Mercury. That's three leads, not a top priority though. My priorities are finding out more about that crazy, telekinetic car chase and getting that machine back from *The Superiors*!"

Jasmine and Lucian both nodded in agreement. The people controlling those cars were *powerful*. They would make a perfect addition to the team, or a perfect enemy.

Arion and Jasmine both left the room which allowed Lucian to do whatever he wanted.

He met up with Meredith in Venice, Italy. "It makes me uneasy being back in Italy," he said. They were both wearing civilian clothes and Lucian ate spaghetti at one of Italy's finest restaurants, Meredith simply drank whatever they had.

"The ocean is so...pure and perfect here. I love it. Was

it really necessary to get spaghetti? That waiter hates you already, just because of that."

"Sorry," he said. He waved his hand and the spaghetti flattened itself and expanded until it was a small, plate-sized pizza. Meredith laughed.

"You need to watch where you use your powers and in front of who," she whispered.

"So do you," he said. She looked down at her glass and realized that it was swirling in a whirlpool.

"Sorry!" she said. She chugged the water and set the glass down.

"You look beautiful, you know?"

"Thanks. Is this the perfect date that you promised me? The one that no *normal* girl could have?"

"I see too many couples around here for it to be unique. We'll get to that *after* the superhero business dies down. Cool?"

"Definitely. Do you want to see Mystica?"

"See the place that my girlfriend is destined to rule?

Wouldn't miss it for the world."

78. <u>CIRCE</u>

After Arion had returned and told Jasmine and Lucian the news about this super speedster, Jasmine decided to get some air. She strolled through the industrial area of Mississauga. She was looking for crime, looking for anything where a superhero could be needed. Hyperion was nowhere to be found—as usual—Lucian and Meredith were in Italy, Arion was probably somewhere with Thalia. She turned and punched the nearest thing to her. The bricks shattered from her blow.

"Never liked that wall, anyway," she muttered to herself.

She thought back to her dream, the one when her dad went into her mind. She couldn't help but think about what he had said: You're a pawn in something much bigger than yourself or your stupid little superhero squad. There are much greater forces at work right now Jasmine, much bigger than me or you or that little do-gooder that you are in love with. She shook the thought out of her head. *He was just trying to scare her, no more, no less.*

She was so busy trying to push thoughts out of her head that she barely even felt whatever hit her in the back of her head.

Jasmines eyes barely fluttered open. She was lying on a cold stone floor and her head was throbbing. She sat up and took in her surroundings. The room that she was in had a bed, a toilet and a small window with bars on it. The room was maybe 10 feet by 11 feet. "Hello!" she called out.

*A man appeared in front of her in a flash of purple light—the same way that her dad teleports. He was wearing a black trench coat with black pants and a black shirt. His skin was deathly pale. "**Pyrolineum**!" she screamed, raising her hands towards him. Nothing happened. "That's not possible! What the hell is happening!? Who are you!?" she demanded.*

*"Oh, my dear, Circe." The man shook his head. "You don't have your powers anymore." He held out his palm. "**Pyrolineum**!" His hand caught fire and a little fireball, swirled maybe two inches above his palm. "I have them."*

She immediately reached for her ear to signal her friends but he held out his index finger and his thumb. He had something in-between them. It was silver and about the size of a blueberry. "No," she whispered. He dropped it into his other flaming hand and they both watched her communicator burn and melt.

"I can't have you escape yet, my dear. I needed to put your abilities to the test during that stupid car chase. I needed to know *who* I wanted. The one *he* cares for the most. That just happened to be you. Your telekinesis has already amplified mine by the hundreds!"

"You can't do this!" she yelled. "Or..." her voice faltered.

"Or *what!*? You can't do anything without your powers. Now you're just a scared, little, girl." He smiled cruelly and walked away, leaving Jasmine lying down on the bed, doing something that she hadn't done in a long time. She cried into her pillow.

Chapter XI: Powers

79. Titan

"And then he just zoomed off, faster than light?" Thalia asked, in awe just as Arion finished telling her the story. Arion nodded grimly. Thalia didn't say anything for about thirty seconds. "That is amazing!"

"Not really, sweetheart. This is difficult. Hyperion is faster than me but he's on the right side. This guy can do whatever he wants, wherever he wants and no one can catch him. If we get a lead on him, it'll be gone the next day."

"I know what you mean. How do you find a guy that's spent so much time running—no pun intended—away from everywhere and everything." Arion smiled. He really did love her.

They were lying down on her bed, facing each other. She was wearing extremely short shorts and a purple tank top—Jasmine's favourite colour. He mentally scolded himself. *Stop that!* He screamed in his mind. *You're with Thalia!* She kissed him for a few seconds. "Don't worry. You'll always be the fastest in my books."

"You taste like cinnamon," he muttered, eyes still closed.

She laughed. "Thank you?" she said it as if it was a question, debating whether she should say it or not. "I need a favour."

"Just name it, beautiful," he said, opening his eyes and sitting up.

"You have an endless memory, right?"

"Technically it's eidetic, but yeah." She shook her head, the grin was still on her face though. "Why?"

"Well I was wondering...if you read a book..."

"I could remember every single word in the book and be able to recite the book perfectly without a heartbeat's hesitation. Where are you going with this?"

"Could you...read an English-Spanish dictionary?" She looked up at him, hope in her nearly glowing, green eyes.

"You think that I could learn a language by reading a dictionary and remembering everything from it?"

"I think that it's worth a shot." Thalia changed into jeans and put a sweater over the tank top and before she could even blink they were standing outside the Brampton Library, a giant brown-bricked building. "I swear, I will never get used to that!"

It took about ten minutes to find the foreign language section and three hours for Arion to read one English-Spanish dictionary, one English dictionary and one Spanish dictionary, twice each at super speed.

"**You look absolutely beautiful, right now, Thalia,**" he said in fluent Spanish.

"**Thanks,**" she said, her cheeks turning red.

He switched to English. "Now the real question. Why did you want me to learn Spanish?" he asked, starting an English-German dictionary.

"Well...I wanted you to meet my mom and she's from the Dominican Republic and..." her voice faltered.

"Let me guess, you want me to honour her in her native language while—also in Spanish—ask her for permission to date you or something?" he asked absentmindedly, not even looking up from his book.

When he did look up, she looked shocked. "Fast, strong and psychic?"

"I prefer telepathic, actually." His stomach began to churn as he immediately thought of Jasmine. "Something is wrong," he said.

"What?" Thalia's smile faded.

"Not with us. With Jasmine. I...I can feel it."

"Arion?" He heard through his communicator, it was Velocity. Arion knew what was coming. He closed his eyes and took a deep breath. **"Jasmine is missing."**

"What do you mean, missing, Velocity?" he demanded through gritted teeth.

"She hasn't been checking in hourly and her communicator was just destroyed."

"Dispatch the team!" he whispered harshly. "Send them to The Central, now!"

"I'll get right on that, Titan."

"Are you good getting home?" he asked Thalia. She nodded. "Jasmine is missing." He saw something in her eyes that he saw whenever he mentioned Jasmine. Jealousy.

"Bye," she whispered.

80. QUANTUM

Lucian flew Meredith to where her island used to be and dropped her from just a few feet above the water and she landed on it, feet first as if it was solid. After about 3 seconds a 5 yard circle of water began to glow a brilliant blue, as did her skin.

"Meredith?" he called out slowly. The circle that she was standing on simply disappeared. It was as if it was never there. Meredith's skin dimmed down to normal just as she fell into the hole. Lucian angled himself and soared after her. He was going crazy, trying to speed up to catch her but she was...laughing. He couldn't tell why until they emerged from the hole into a huge area. It was almost an ocean...under the ocean. There were trees and mountains and land. All underwater. It was then that he got the call from Velocity.

"She's what!?" Lucian demanded once they reached The Central. "Has she been kidnapped? Did she just leave? Was she in some sort of accident that could've destroyed her communicator?" He knew that it was nearly impossible to destroy those communicators; he had made sure of that.

They were sitting around their 'dining room' table. It was mostly used for team meetings, 5 chairs around a small, circular table. Only one was empty. "Velocity, any news?" he asked.

"I am checking the security cameras around the building." They waited a few seconds. Meredith tapped her foot repeatedly against the ground. He took her hand under the table and her foot stopped shaking. **"This really isn't good."**

"Really?" Hyperion asked sarcastically.

"Indeed." The center of the table, just before the edge spiraled like a large camera lens and there was a screen on it. Arion raised his hands and a holographic projection came up. On the video was a guy walking down the street, not too far from The Central. Lucian had been there before. The man was walking with a limp and a walking stick.

The man lifted up the walking stick and brought it down hard on her head. She crumpled to the ground. He picked her up and slung her over his shoulder. Immediately after he touched her a wave of light washed over them and the screen turned black. When it came back on, they were gone.

"What. Did. He. Do. To. Her?" Arion asked Velocity through gritted teeth.

"All that we can currently tell is that this man has taken her through some sort of teleportation that is nearly identical to that of Jasmine's father, Immortales." Arion flinched when he heard that name.

"We're going to need help to look for her," Lucian decided. "We're fast but... we need faster." Lucian looked up at Arion hopefully.

"No," Arion said after a few seconds. Everyone looked

at him. "He's unpredictable! The last time he was here he stole our stuff, worth well over 10,000 dollars and my wallet."

Hyperion spoke up, "It's for Jasmine. We should give him a chance."

"He said that you knew how to call him, right?" Lucian asked.

"Yeah," Arion agreed with a sigh, pulling out his cell phone. "Just...give me a bit. You guys start looking for her." He was gone before anyone could protest.

81.   CIRCE

Somewhere in between her spontaneous crying fits, Jasmine somehow fell asleep in the cold cell. She awoke to even colder water being thrown on her head. She sat up so quickly that she started to see spots, although that could've been hypothermia. She couldn't tell.

The man from earlier, the one who stole her powers, was standing at the bars of her cell holding an empty bucket.

"Wakey, wakey," he joked with a crooked smile. This time someone else was standing beside him, though. Even though the last time she had seen him, he was pointing a gun to the back of her head and she had only gotten a glimpse of him. He had a black cape, white suit and a black utility belt with a black mask with big red eyes and a red crosshair on a black circle in the middle of his chest.

"Blank?" she asked. Her voice was raspy and her throat, dry. The man beside blank raised his arms and Jasmine flew against the wall above her bed.

"Prisoners do not speak unless spoken to," the man said. Blank moved with blinding—yet human—speed. Good, she thought, we don't need another superhuman enemy. He had one sword sideways behind the man's neck and another one in front of his neck, the point not even an inch from his flesh. Jasmine could've sworn that she saw a flash of green behind them but quickly blamed it on the fact that she probably had hypothermia.

"You idiot!" Blank yelled. "They will come looking for her! They will leave no stone unturned! They will find you!"

"Oh, I'm counting on it!" The man spat. "I've seen the

future! There is only one way to protect the world!" he whispered something into Blanks ear.

"Dad...no. You can't!" Blank begged. *Did he say...dad?* Jasmine asked herself.

"After what her father did to your mother, she deserves it!"

"But mom is still alive!"

"But she's paralyzed! She would be better off dead!" he sounded as if he was ready to cry.

"Still here," Jasmine muttered, teeth chattering. Blanks dad was suddenly thrown backwards. Jasmine thought that he had teleported at first but when Arion appeared in front of her, with the bars to her cell bent aside, she knew exactly what was happening.

"Oh my GOD! Dad?" Blank screamed just as the rest of the team (and some other guy) burst into the room. Then she realized what Blank was really screaming at. He ran towards his dad. His dad was across the room, hanging on a wall...with a metal pole through the center of his chest.

82.   TITAN

Arion had called Max with something that he hadn't noticed right away. After Max took his wallet—which he was still extremely mad about—he entered his number into his phone. Before Arion *or* Velocity even noticed.

Within 20 minutes, Max had found Jasmine and reported it back to the rest of the team. Arion got there before anyone, even Max, and as soon as he got there, he pushed Jasmines abductor aside with one hand. Jasmine had one cell out of four. They were in the basement of a house in Pennsylvania.

He used all of his strength to bend the bars of Jasmines cell and just as he was about to help her, he saw the man against the wall with the pole through his chest. "No," Arion whispered examining his hands.

He ran over to the man who gripped Blanks hands tightly. "I love you and your mother. Always remember that. Live your life. This was the only way..." his eyes began to close.

"DAD!" Blank yelled, he ripped off his mask to show a young, Hispanic face but Arion recognized it from the files when they were searching for teammates. Benito Suarez, son of Artemis, the superhero from The Titans.

The man opened his eyes just barely, "Promise me! He. Will. Be. SUMMONED!" In between each word he took a deep raspy breath.

"I promise, Dad. I...I love you."

"I lo..." Arion heard one last thu-bump inside the man's chest. His hand went limp in Blank's. A mixture of colours, dozens of them, erupted from the man. Two flew into Max, three or four of them flew into Jasmine and the rest went crazy, trying to escape from the prison. Blank pulled out one of his swords slowly. He backed up, away from Arion.

"You...you killed him!" He screamed. He threw the sword into the air and on the flip it morphed into a pistol.

"I didn't...I'm...I'm sorry! I didn't mean to!" Blank let off four shots but Arion stood his ground.

"I hate you!" Blank yelled as three of the bullets sunk into Arion's chest. The other one hit him in the stomach. He fell backwards towards the ground. Jasmine screamed so loudly, that it would've hurt his ears if he wasn't dying. That was the last sound that he heard before everything went black.

83.   <u>QUANTUM</u>

"Hyperion!" Lucian shouted, "Get him to Area 02! Now!" Hyperion and Arion were gone in a flash of yellow light leaving Jasmine, Meredith, Max and Lucian facing Blank. Blank quickly pulled out a sword from one of the crossing sheaths on his back and with a flip of the pistol, he was holding another.

Max charged at him at super speed but at the last second, Blank ducked and slashed both of his legs. Lucian heard the echo of his bones cracking. Due to his momentum, he slid all the way to the other side of the room, into Jasmine's old cell, crying out in pain.

Out of the ground, some old pipes cracked the cement and water erupted from them. Blank quickly flipped over it and brought the hilt of his sword down hard on Meredith's head and she crumpled to the ground, the water residing.

Jasmine and Lucian stood side by side, looking at this human kid that had just gotten 4 super powered people out of his way in under one minute.

"Magical weapons," he said, spinning the sword in his right hand. "*Your* mom charmed them for mine. Able to take on the form of any weapon and able to pierce anything. *Including* your boyfriend."

Jasmine—obviously with her powers back—flew full speed at Blank. In one swift motion, he hit her in the face with a war-like hammer, knocking her out cold and leaving her sprawled out on the floor a few feet away.

Lucian lifted his hand in concentration, trying to rearrange the molecules in the weapons. They wouldn't budge, they vibrated slightly and glowed bright silver.

"Ah, ah, ah," he said waving the sword in a no gesture. "Anything inside the weapon or the weapon itself isn't affected by any powers." The sword morphed into a pistol and Lucian instinctively put up a force field. Time seemed to slow down as Lucian watched the bullet fly through the force field and straight through his heart. He looked up and saw Blank running the other way. Then everything went black.

CHAPTER XII: MISTAKES

84.   CIRCE

*J*asmine was the first to wake up. She sat up and rubbed her head and already found a small bump that hurt to the touch. Blank was long gone because she couldn't sense him telepathically—or that might've been because of the bump, she couldn't tell.

She ran to the closest person to her, Meredith, and shook her awake. She tried not to look at Blank's dad.

"Huh? What?" she sat up quickly and then grabbed her head. "Ow, ow, oww. What the hell happened?"

"Blank happened. You good to stand?" Meredith nodded and stood. "Wake Lucian, I'll get the other guy. Area 02, okay?" Again Meredith nodded and jogged to Lucian.

Jasmine had never seen Max before then. At first glance, Jasmine gasped. He was hot. He had short black hair, gelled up and he was skinny, not too tall, 5-foot-11 maybe. She shook him and his eyes snapped open. His lime green eyes seemed to spark and then an electrical surge erupted from his body and sent her flying back onto her prison-bed.

"Jeeze," he said, scrambling to get up. "I didn't even...I don't even...what was that?" Max started bouncing from one foot to the other tapping his hand nervously on his pants.

"It's okay," Jasmine assured him. He continued to tap his hand against his leg. "Are you okay?" she asked him.

His fingers stopped tapping and he looked her in the eye and nodded. "ADHD," he replied. "Hyperactivity comes with the speed."

"I knew someone with it back at the—" she stopped herself. She was going to say foster home but chose against it. "I can tell. You're impulsive...I like that." He gave her a devilish smile before nodding and walking out of the cell. "Your legs," she noted, "they're okay?"

"Speed healing also comes with the super speed." Once they emerged from the cell, they saw Meredith dragging Lucian with one arm swung around her shoulder. Jasmine told Max where Area 02 was he picked Lucian up and left with a faint sonic boom. Jasmine and Meredith followed as fast as they could.

Once they arrived at Area 02, they were stuck in the

waiting room as Lucian and Arion were being treated. Jasmine paced while Hyperion and Max tried to determine who was faster without actually racing.

"When Blank's dad died," Meredith said after 20 minutes of silence, "Jasmine and Max were hit with those weird lights but no one else. Blank was there, Me, Lucian...none of us got hit, just you two."

"All of the powers that he stole were released I think. That's what happened! That's why I got my powers back! But...Max?"

"I always felt like I was missing something. He tapped his foot quickly on the ground until it moved at super speed. Stealing, speed, tricking...always been easy but there are other aspects to Hermes..."

"Maybe your dad—" Max's gaze made Jasmine stop talking. But he sighed.

"Sorry. You're right. I need to find my parents," he decided.

"You don't know where they are?" Meredith asked.

"It's worse than that. I don't even know *who* they are."

85. <u>TITAN</u>

Arion was having a sweet dream. Titan was celebrity judging a swimsuit competition which just happened to have Thalia and Jasmine in it. Just as he was choosing the winner, his dream morphed.

The next thing he knew, he was sitting in Mr. Shuster's class, back at school. Arion heard a horn—from a car or another vehicle. It was blaring, loudly and getting closer. In not even one second a school bus crashed through the roof of the school. Arion snapped into action immediately. He jumped into the air and caught the bus and somehow, he could fly. He flew the bus outside and put it onto the street.

The entire student body began piling out of the school to see the commotion. Arion only heard one sentence that made his heart skip a beat.

"ARION ZIMMERMAN IS TITAN!" a student yelled.

"He killed that guy!" one said, pointing at the bus. Arion didn't even care about people seeing him using his powers. He ran to the bus and ripped off the door. He climbed in and lifted the drivers head off of the steering wheel and the horn stopped blaring. He looked at the man's face and saw Blank's dad staring back at him with cold dead eyes.

Arion scrambled out of the bus, shocked by the man. "I hate you," someone said behind him. He spun to see Thalia staring at him. There was fear in her eyes, hate, and anger. "I hate you! Murderer! I hate you! Murderer!" Everyone else began to chant too.

He felt his eyes beginning to burn, heating up and he couldn't take his eyes off of Thalia. "NO!" he cried. His eyes exploded with solar vision disintegrating Thalia and all of the other students in 10 seconds.

Arion took off into the sky with so much force that the ground cracked. He floated aimlessly in space, staring at the earth until his solar vision came back. The beams hit the earth with such intensity that it glowed red. A few more seconds and it began to crack, spewing red light from them. "NO!" he yelled as the earth exploded. Jasmine, Meredith, Hyperion, Lucian and Max appeared in front of him.

"You aren't one of us," Jasmine spat. "You're not even remotely human. Freak!" Jasmine unleased a telekinetic blast, Meredith blasted him with unseen water, Hyperion blasted him with light, Lucian blasted him with energy and—the most surprising—Max shot him with an arc of green electricity. The power from the blows were too much and he flew backwards into the core of the sun.

Arion awoke with a jolt. When he opened his eyes there was a doctor looking at him from a few feet above him. He had white skin and blue eyes but everything else was covered.

"Good as new," the doctor said. He held a long pair of tweezers and a metal pan. The metal pan had bloodied water inside of it, nearly filled up to the brim and four crushed silver bullets.

He looked down and saw that his shirt was off. He was wearing the pants, boots and belt of his costume but everything else was stripped away. The doctor walked out and three seconds later, the whole team—minus Lucian, plus Max—wandered into the room with his dad. He tried to sit up but grunted. He looked down and saw four holes in his torso closing up slowly.

Jasmine immediately launched into a story about what happened after he was shot and he listened intently. "Blank took on all four of you...and walked away without a scratch?" They all nodded. "Lucian?"

"Unconscious in the next ro—" Jasmine stopped mid-speech and so did everything else. Arion knew exactly what had happened, something was activated in his speed. Max walked through the team and sat down on Arion's bed.

"How did you...?" Arion couldn't get it out.

"I just kinda focused my speed on us, I guess." Max smiled.

"Why?" Arion asked.

"I need to go." Max frowned at the ground.

"Why? Stay with us. Join the team!" Arion pleaded.

"I'm not ready for that yet."

"Are you sure?" Arion asked. He nodded. "You know that you always have us, right?"

"Yeah. I got it." Arion watched as Max broke through the sound barrier in one step.

"—om," Jasmine continued as if nothing had happened. The only thing that made them aware that he was gone was that their ears were ringing. "Where'd Max go?" she asked.

"Out," Arion whispered. "If you guys don't mind...I need a moment alone with my dad." Everyone piled out of the room except for

Arthur. After all of the holes had closed up, Arion sat up on the bed and his dad sat next to him.

"It wasn't your fault," he immediately said as if he had read Arion's mind. He punched straight through the heart-rate monitor.

"Yes it was!" he shouted, "I...I..." his voice faltered until it was barely a whisper, "I killed him."

"Arion, it was an accident! Everyone makes mistakes!"

"You told me to be careful with my powers. Not to let anger and fear cloud my judgement. I killed him! Me!" Arion cried into his dad's shoulder. "I'm never ever taking another life again. Not for as long as I live. It will never be by my hand. Ever."

"Don't worry," he whispered, "You won't have to."

86. QUANTUM

Lucian was getting sick of having the same dream nearly every night. There were the same three figures as every other night. The three of them shimmered into Arion, Lucian and Jasmine, nothing different happened.

"He has been summoned!"

Lucian woke with a start and standing next to his bed was Max. "I'm going to go find my parents..." he said, his voice trailing off. "The others don't know you're awake, yet they're with Arion. Just thought you should know. I'll be seeing you."

Just as he turned to run, Lucian grabbed his arm. "Wait...you're missing something." Lucian snapped his fingers and a nearly flat circle of energy erupted around Max's waist, similar to Arion's costume changer. One moved upwards and the other moved downwards and in a few seconds, he was wearing a red long-sleeved shirt with metallic yellow highlights and sleeves with metallic red pants. The last to come in was a helmet that covered his whole face and had a small visor where his eyes were.

He pushed a button on the side and the mask dispersed into the shoulders and back of the suit. "This is..."

"An exact replica of your dad's costume. It has a communicator built in but isn't activated yet. You can decide on that one."

"I don't think I should be wearing this..." he said looking down at it.

"It's not who wore the suit before you...it's who's
wearing the suit now. Remember that, Max." He nodded
and blurred out.

A few seconds later, the rest of the team poured in—
minus Arion. As soon as Hyperion walked through the door,
he was gone in a flash of light.

"Nice guy," Lucian muttered. Meredith hugged him
while Jasmine stood there awkwardly.

"Arion's all healed up," Jasmine said.

"Where is he?" Lucian asked—even though Max had
told him everything.

"Next room, with his dad."

"Why?" he asked. "What's the prob—?"

Then he heard something in the back of his mind saying: **"Don't worry, I'll explain later,"** and he couldn't help

following the instructions. Jasmine smirked but he couldn't even say anything.

87. CIRCE

Jasmine had been practicing the mind-manipulation ever since she first discovered it. Sometimes she would ask someone to do something and they'd literally drop everything and do it for her.

"How did you do that?" Lucian demanded. They were wandering down the halls of The Central. Meredith had gone back to Mystica, Hyperion was nowhere to be found and Arion was at home.

"Do what?" Jasmine asked innocently.

"How the hell did you make me shut up!? Nobody can do that!" he yelled. Then his face turned bright red, probably realizing that he had just insulted himself. "Not what I meant!"

"Magic," she said, laughing.

"That was not magic. You didn't even recite a spell! It was…it was telepathy, wasn't it?" Jasmine was silent. "Who else knows?"

"Just Arion," she said.

Of course, she heard him think to himself. *Who else would know?* She turned and slammed him into the nearest wall.

"Don't go there, *Lieber,* don't you *dare* go there!" She held his collar in one hand and called out, "**Pyrolineum**," causing her other hand to erupt into flames. Her face became bright red and her ears became hot.

"That's cute," he said. He started to sing, "Titan and Circe sitting in a tree, K-I-S-S-I-N—" he didn't even get to finish before he got a fire ball to the face. "Sooo not fair!" he said coughing smoke.

"You asked for it," she muttered as she walked away from him.

You hide too much, he mentally sent from behind her, *why don't you just tell him how you feel, Jaz?* She flew off so quickly that the walls cracked from the force.

A few hours later she was sitting on top of the CN Tower's railing with her legs dangling off of the side, looking out over Toronto. She heard a familiar whoosh of air behind *her, "All alone?"*

"Hey, Arion," she said without turning around. "Maybe just a bit."

"Why don't you just conjure up some friends or some-thing?"

Jasmine laughed. "I'm not that powerful yet, sweet-heart." She winced as soon as she said it.

"It's okay," he said.

Eager to change the subject, Jasmine said, "How are you doing with...everything."

"I'm a wreck. I wouldn't even be going anywhere but you were here and..." his voice faltered. "I needed a friend."

"Just a friend?" she asked. "Not a girlfriend?" He shook his head and she looked down. "If I fell...would you catch me?" she asked.

"You can fly..." he said, not knowing what she was thinking.

"Not anymore!" she snapped her fingers and leaped off of the statue, laughing. Arion waited until she was about 10 feet above the ground and he super-sped down and caught her on the sidewalk surrounding the building. He caught her

in his arms and brought her back to the top of the tower within a second.

He set her back down at the top and she looked him in the eye. "Absolutely spectacular!" she cried out, clapping.

"Thanks...I think," he muttered. He sat down on the ledge beside her. "Jaz, I have something to tell y—" he stopped mid-sentence as if listening to something.

Jasmine sighed, Of course, she thought to herself, as soon as something good happens.

"There's a disturbance here, in Toronto," he groaned. He stood up and extended his hand to her. "It'll only take the two of us. Let's go."

She took his hand and in a whoosh, they were a couple kilometers away from the CN Tower.

"I will never get tired of that," Jasmine whispered. After a few seconds, she quickly let go of Arion's hand, as if just realizing that she was still holding onto it.

"Okay," Arion said rubbing his hands together. "We got Arc, Pixie and Nexus. Think we could—" he stopped and grabbed Jasmine in his arms, crouching with his body shielding her as an SUV dropped from the sky and crashed down

on top of them.

It bounced off of Arion's back and didn't even touch Jasmine. "Nice one," she whispered.

"It's what I do. At least now we know where the action is, right?"

"Yeah," she said, eyeing him closely. "I guess we do."

88. <u>TITAN</u>

Their battle was done within ten minutes. Nexus and Arc got away but they captured Pixie. She was needed for questioning.

Once they got to Area 25, Corbin put Pixie in the same interrogation room that Lucian was in when he was Ares. "All yours," Arion said to Corbin.

"You're going in without me," he said. "I'll whisper the questions under my breath, you interrogate her. You're way more terrifying than some old guy in a suit."

"Why do you guys want the machine? And why haven't you used

it yet?" Arion asked once he went into the room.

"I don't have to tell you anything. I want a lawyer!" Pixie barked. Arion gripped her neck and lifted her a few inches off of the ground.

"Do I look like a cop to you?"

"No...powers..." she gasped.

He dropped her to the ground. "Power dampeners don't affect me. What do you want with the machine," he said. He flashed his eyes yellow which took a lot of energy out of him. Maybe the power dampener, did affect him. He didn't even know if his solar vision would work but she didn't need to know that.

"We want more people with powers!" she yelled, crawling backwards in fear.

"The professor said that it may not even work. What makes you so sure?"

"It's been used before!" she yelled.

"But the professor said——" Pixie interrupted him.

"YOU THINK THAT I DON'T KNOW WHAT THE PROFESSOR SAID!?" she screamed at him, standing up and getting in his face. "Where do you think I got my powers from? That machine tainted people's genes and random objects. I was in the middle of getting a flu shot when the vaccination was tainted! The opening to your friend's godly dimension, was opened by the machine. Your girlfriend's sorcery? Activated by the machine! That's what lead her father to her! The Prime Minister knew that it wouldn't work but he forced it! He created over 75% of these so-called Evolutionaries!

"We know that you killed our employer, Mr. Suarez, but his son is doing just fine! We're fixing the machine, making it better. We can do it and we're going to. After the machine is activated, I'll be disposable. I don't mind...it'll be for a good cause. You're fighting us like we're the bad guys when the real one is sitting in his neat little office in Ottawa." She sat back down hard on the bed and turned away.

Arion turned and walked out of the room. Jasmine and Corbin were standing outside, shocked. "Where are they?" he asked Jasmine.

"All that I got was that she was telling the truth...I can't get that deep."

"Can you make her to tell us?" Arion asked.

"No. It's like her brain is made out of...rubber or something. I can get a vibe but I can't get the full story. It's like reading every third or fourth word. Enrique was employing them?"

"We're going to find out. Corbin," Arion said, turning his attention to him. "Set up a meeting between Lucian, Jasmine, The Prime Minister and I. And keep it off the books. If he refuses, tell him I'll break down his goddamned door myself!"

89. QUANTUM

After his dispute with Jasmine, Lucian went to Mystica to meet up with Meredith. She gave him a place to rest for the night and he did.

Once Lucian woke up, Meredith rode in on a *unicorn*. At first he thought that he was dreaming but then he realized that it was very real. The unicorn was a very light shade of yellow, almost white and had a lemon-yellow mane running down its head and the same coloured tail and...corn? Horn? He didn't know what to call the point on its head.

"That will *never* be normal," Lucian said, shaking his head.

Meredith hopped off of the unicorn. "Unicorns are surprisingly strong and they ride rainbows," she said happily. "Her name is Astra, bright as a star. She's been helping me build my kingdom."

"My girlfriend, Queen of Mystica, a magical island submerged underwater that no one will believe existed," he said making a makeshift camera with his hands. Just as the wave of water was about to wash over him, he turned and clapped. The wave immediately turned into hundreds of sugar cubes. Best part about having a super-girlfriend. She doesn't playfully punch you in the arm and say: *Stop it!* Nah, she'll throw a thousand gallons of water at you. "I hope unicorns eat sugar cubes," he said, "don't horses?"

Meredith nodded. "Now can I properly show you around?" she asked.

"If you insist, beautiful," Meredith blushed and led them away from *Astra the Unicorn.* "I could help you build all of this in not even a day, you know that, right?"

"I want my people to know that I actually put some work into it, not relied on my boyfriend." She nudged him with her elbow.

"People? There are people here?" he asked.

"Not yet. Centurion told me—" she started but Lucian interrupted.

"Centurion?" he asked.

"The one who watches over Mystica in-between rulers. He told me that when I am ready to rule, when I take charge. The people will come to me, they will be drawn to me—I mean Mystica."

"Uh-huh," Lucian said nodding. "So...all of this is yours? You own Atlantis? Camelot? It's yours?"

"Yep," she said. Lucian heard a ferocious roar coming from behind them. "It's a bear," she said, "and he's hurt."

Meredith darted deeper into the forest and Lucian followed as closely behind as possible. In a few minutes, they reached a small opening. There was a cracked tree and the bear was lying on the ground, bleeding and crying out in pain.

"What happened?" Lucian asked.

"Probably one of the dinosaurs," Meredith said.

"Dinosaurs!?" Lucian demanded.

"Huh? What? Nothing. Lift him up onto a platform." Lucian did as he was told and Meredith hopped onto the platform beside it. Lucian flew alongside them until they were high enough. Meredith pointed at a small pond not even two football fields away. Lucian flew them as fast as he could. Once they reached the pond Lucian saw how beautiful it really was. The pond was perfectly round and about the size of a swimming pool. There was a perfect cliff with a perfect waterfall that lead into the pond. The pond had a *natural* fountain in the middle spouting water back into the pond.

"Get over it!" Meredith yelled and Lucian snapped out of it. "Keep the platform steady and lower him gently into the water." Lucian did as he was told and suddenly the bear was completely submerged.

"Can he breathe?" he asked. Meredith ignored him and she was counting in barely a whisper.

"30! Bring him up!" When Lucian brought him up there was a bear about a third of the size of the 300 pound bear that just went under. It had the same black nose and brown fur. The only difference is that he was simply younger. "Go on, buddy," Meredith coaxed him once Lucian brought him back above land.

The bear—whom was taller than Meredith not even a minute ago—was now at her waist. He rubbed his head against her leg, in appreciation. "No problem, go on now. Be careful!" the bear trotted off back into the forest.

"The fountain of youth?" Lucian demanded.

"I told you Mystica was a magical place! Just wait till you see what is on top of the cliff!" A disk about 10 inches all around, emerged out of the fountain of youth and Meredith hopped on it, floating upwards. She looked back at Lucian, "You coming or what?"

Over the cliff was absolutely amazing. There were animals everywhere. Some of them were humanoid, others were just everyday animals that you'd see in a forest and they were all helping to build a huge palace.

"Meredith—" he was in awe, he could barely speak. "This is absolutely amazing! Do the animals understand you?"

"Yeah, they do...or at least they're learning to."

"This is so..." he couldn't even find the words for it. After a few seconds, he finally decided on, "awesome!"

"Thanks! Want to see inside?" That's when they got the call to report to The Central.

CHAPTER XIII: THE SUPERIORS

90. CIRCE

*A*ll five members of the team met up at The Central within the hour. *"A meet up with the Prime Minister?"* Lucian scoffed. *"Why?"*

Jasmine told everyone the full story and Lucian was completely silent throughout the whole thing. *"You're telling me,"* Meredith began, *"That the Prime Minister created 75% of the evolutionary community?"*

Jasmine nodded. *"And tried to create more."*

"And he opened the portal to the realms of the gods...and your sorcery," Lucian muttered. *"He helped create this team whether he wanted to or not. All he wanted was to become a super powered guy. He's already the one of the most powerful men in the world—arguably—and he would be way more powerful with super powers. I say yes to the talk."*

"Good," Arion said. *"Corbin set the meeting for as soon as possible."*

"It's always a pleasure, Guardians. What brings my favourite superhero team to my office?" They were standing in

front of the Prime Minister's desk and he sat behind it. Arion blurred closer to the desk and back to where he was standing before.

"That is what brings us here," Jasmine declared, pointing at the picture that Arion had just put on the desk.

"Oh yes," the Prime Minister croaked. *"I heard that this was stolen. What a pity."*

"With all due respect, Mr. Prime Minister..." Jasmine said sweetly, *"cut the crap."*

"I beg your pardon?" he growled.

"We know that you made it," Arion claimed.

"We know that you activated it at least *once,"* Lucian chimed in.

"And we know," Jasmine said, *"that you have created at least 75% of the Evolutionaries in the world."*

The Prime Minister's smile slowly faded. *"These are some bold accusations, don't you think?"* Jasmine saw his finger move under the desk. A few seconds later, two men in black suits and sunglasses walked into the room. *"Mr. Johan and Mr. Solomon will escort you out."*

"Actually," Arion decided, *"I don't think we're done*

here." Before Arion even took one step forward, the suits were at each of his sides holding him back.

"Listen to me, very closely, Titan," he spat the name as if it was a swear word. He got up and limped until he was right in his face. "You're going to stop poking your nose in my business. Do you understand me?"

"No," Jasmine spoke up, "he won't. We won't, because no matter who you think you are, if you dare commit a crime in this country or even on this planet. You'll answer to us. Is that understood Mr. Prime Minister?" The Prime Minister raised his hands and the guards let go of Arion. He walked— limped—up to Jasmine.

"Bold words for such a pitiful little girl," he clucked. "Don't think for one second that I forgot who your father was. I know that you'll turn out just like him...it's in his blood."

"People change," she admitted.

"Oh, yes, they do," he whispered. "Get me my machine back or consider your superhero careers terminated, am I clear?"

"Crystal," Jasmine grumbled.

"Good," he said, his smile coming back. "Now if it's not too much trouble...get the hell out of my building! I have a phone call to make with a Mr. Suarez."

91.　<u>TITAN</u>

"You don't even know how much I felt like punching that guy right in the face," Arion said.

"That would've been an act of terrorism," Thalia retaliated. Arion told her about his entire day and how fast it got crazy. He had told her the main things:

1. Jasmine got kidnapped.

2. He had killed a guy, Suarez who is actually the criminal mastermind behind almost everything supervillain related.

3. Blank/Kid Suarez took out the entire team single-handedly

4. The stolen machine created all the heroes

5. It was the Prime Minister's machine

6. The Prime Minister was working with or for Suarez too.

"So..." he said once he was done. "How was your day?"

"It was good...I guess," she paused for a second. "NO! N-n-n-n-no, wait! This is way too much to process! You killed a guy, almost got killed, saved Jasmine, made enemies with the Prime Minister? AND got shot?"

"It was a rather interesting day," he said. They were strolling through the park, the same park that they had had their first real date after years of flirting.

"You're an amazing guy, you know that?" Arion blinked a few times.

"Wait...what? You're not...mad or scared or something."

"It was an accident, right?" he nodded slowly. "Then there is no shame in that. Just...be more careful. Okay?"

"Yeah, sure thing," he said.

"Now," she said. She seemed nervous, eagerly trying to change the subject. Then she asked randomly, "have you ever X-rayed me before?"

"You know what?" Arion said in a mocking voice. "I think I'm hearing a cry for help right about now." He super-sped off and halfway to the soccer field in front of them.

"Are you kidding me!?" she yelled. "ARION! GET BACK HERE!" He just laughed and kept appearing in different places.

"It's nice to just...relax, you know?" he asked her. They were standing on the edge of the Space Needle in Seattle, looking down at the city. "You're probably the only thing that really makes me feel...human."

"And you connect me to my inner superhero."

"Or villain," he whispered to her. She giggled and pushed him away.

Arion tilted his head, listening to something miles away. "They're setting up the machine," he whispered before taking Thalia home and rushing all the way to The Central.

92. QUANTUM

"You didn't say *anything*?" Meredith asked Lucian as they flew back to Mystica.

"I'm not the kind of guy that starts a fight with the Prime Minister," he retaliated.

"But, I guess you *are* not the type of guy who would let

his friends get chewed out for—" she stopped midsentence when a familiar rainbow-coloured portal swirled to life around them.

Lucian woke up on the cold ground of somewhere that he knew very well. "Aethera," he said aloud. The feeling came back to his arms and legs and he realized that he was holding hands with Meredith who was groggily waking up beside him.

"We have *way* too many magical kingdoms," she muttered, rubbing her head. In a few seconds, his dad and a woman appeared in front of him. His dad wore the same thing that he wore the last few times that they had met. The woman wore a long blue dress.

"Oh, Gods," the woman whispered. She had long blue hair and blue eyes that were rippling with coffee-brown coloured skin. She covered her mouth with her hand and fell to her knees, crying. "I thought...oh my Gods."

Meredith stared at the crying woman. "Who are you?"

"Amphitrite, Goddess of the Ocean, wife of Poseidon. Also...I'm your mother, Meredith."

"Say what now?" Lucian exclaimed.

Lucian wandered off with his father while Meredith left with her mother. "Her mom...is a goddess? Is her dad Poseidon?" he demanded.

"Gods aren't always very...*faithful* to their spouses. Being related by blood means absolutely nothing. For an example, Zeus bore many children although he is married to Hera, also his sister."

"That is disgusting," Lucian mumbled.

"As humans may think," he retaliated.

"I thought I was a God!" Lucian replied.

"But you think like a human," he said, "which makes you no different from them, besides your power. This is the only reason that you have not reached your true godly potential. This is why you need your training."

"That's why I'm here, isn't it?" he asked with a sigh.

"Training?"

"Not yet," his dad said with a chuckle. "I summoned Meredith here through your power again. Her mother had absolutely no idea where she was. Her father was a human and he kidnapped her as a child. You now know that the portal to our worlds were opened by that machine created by the Canadian Prime Minister, which is what showed Amphitrite that Meredith was still alive."

"Wow," Lucian said with a whistle. "So am I going back home?"

"This *is* your home. You'll be sent back to Earth with Meredith when Amphitrite is done talking to her. Do not mention anything of Meredith in front of Poseidon. He...*disagrees* with his wife's demigod children."

"Doesn't he have demigod kids?"

"Ah, yes. But when the men do it, it's considered okay. The women...not so much."

"I see," Lucian said. "When do I have to come back?"

"I'm not sure yet. We're having some problems around

here, as you may know with Ares and a few other gods. It will be resolved *very* soon though."

"Alright," Lucian said slowly. "Did you ever love my mom?"

"Pardon?" his dad asked.

"Mom. Did you love her?" he asked again. "You said Gods think differently than us—I mean them."

"Aye, the Gods do think *and* love differently than mortals, son. I may have loved her...but I knew I could never have been with her. It is forbidden...an ancient law, gods cannot marry humans or live with them. I did not want to turn her into a goddess, she wasn't ready. Never got the chance to be either."

"You mean...the car accident?"

"It was the universe. I was playing a dangerous game, becoming too attached. The universe...well it didn't like that very much. Sent a truck barrelling straight for us. I survived, healed. But your mother...she wasn't strong enough. Now she resides in the—" he stopped talking abruptly but continued walking.

"Where is she, dad?" Lucian begged.

"I shouldn't have said anything," his father said, worried. "I'm sorry."

"She's in the underworld?"

"She's where she was meant to be, Lucian."

"Wait...you mean you never *checked*?"

"Checked what?" his dad asked. He stopped and faced his son.

"You never *checked* to see where she ended up? Never *checked* to see how she was coping with being *dead* and all!? Never!?"

"Son, calm down. I wasn't—" his dad began but was interrupted by someone behind them yelling.

"Lucian!" It was Meredith's voice.

"I'm not your son!" Lucian whispered. "We may have the same powers, same genes, same *blood* but I *am not* your son." Lucians dad nodded just as Meredith came.

"I met my mom!" she yelled, jumping into his arms. His

dad was gone by the time Lucian tried to look at him again.

"I know...I was there," he said in an automatic voice.

"What's wrong?" she asked him, pouting.

"Huh? Nothing," he put on a fake smile. "I'm happy for you, I really am."

Anger creates portals, he heard in his head.

He waved his hand and a swirling portal of red energy appeared in front of them before quickly changing back to the usual rainbow. "We're leaving?" she asked.

"Yeah," he said quietly. "It's time to go. I can send you back here whenever you want though."

Just as he was walked through the other side of the portal, he got a call on his communicator. "Lucian, Meredith...we need you guys now," it was Arion. "Pixie just broke out. We need to get to that machine. *Now!*"

93.   CIRCE

The Prime Minister, The Superiors, Animon, Immortales! They're all connected by one thing," Arion said.

"Suarez," Jasmine finished for him.

"Suarez is dead," Lucian replied.

"He has a son. And he is taking over the operations from what we can tell. If Suarez has all of these villains in his back pocket...there's no telling what he would do."

Jasmine took this moment to tell them about when her father invaded her dream. It seemed like so long ago.

"You're a pawn in something much bigger than yourself or your stupid little superhero squad. There are much greater forces at work right now Jasmine, much bigger than me or you. That is exactly what he said to me."

"This is big. We need to stop this, now."

"The Prime Minister obviously isn't going to help us," Jasmine stated.

"And cows say moo!" Lucian yelled. Everyone looked at him. *"Sorry, thought we were stating the obvious!"*

Arion chuckled which earned a sharp glance from Jasmine. *Sorry,* he whispered in her mind.

"We need to go out and get this machine. It's unstable and could possibly cause just as many deaths as it does supervillains."

"Don't rule out heroes," Meredith said. "There're always heroes."

"Speaking of heroes," she said to Arion, "have you tried Max yet?"

"No answer. No service actually. Like he's in a dead zone."

"Looks like it's just us then," Jasmine whispered.

"When has that ever stopped us, doll?" Hyperion asked.

"Never," Arion said. "It would be nice to have the extra help though."

Everyone muttered their agreements. "We're going to split up," Jasmine said. "Search everywhere."

"Found it!" Arion yelled.

"When did you even leave?" Jasmine demanded.

"He didn't," Hyperion muttered. Arion snapped his fingers and from the center of the table, the holographic screen popped up.

"This is live," Arion said.

A female reporter came into view on the screen. "—here in Toronto where the supervillain team that has come to be known as *The Superiors* is terrorizing the city! Paul, they *have a machine on top of the CN Tower here that is pulsating with energy—" a giant arm swept in front of the camera and the reporter flew into a brick wall down the street. Jasmine saw Arion wince.*

"And to Rage on the scene," grumbled Rage's gruff voice. "Well, Paul, I just wanted to give a shout-out to my fa-vourite superheroes, The Guardians!" He started making mock cheering sounds before he said, "Come and get some," and he punched the camera man while breaking the camera in half, making the screen go black.

After a few seconds of silence, Arion finally spoke up. "You guys ready for this?" Everyone nodded, no one backed down. Meredith held Lucian's hand as they listened to the plan. "Hyperion and I are on civilian evacuation, Jasmine, Lucian, Meredith, you guys are playing offense and we'll get in the fight as soon as we can. Clear?" Everyone nodded. "Alright! What are we waiting for!? Let's go!"

Not even five minutes later, Jasmine was in the battle of her life. Jasmine flew at Huntress but she easily sidestepped, grabbed Jasmine's foot and slammed her into the wall in front of her.

"Bring it on, sister," Huntress said before Jasmine attacked again. Huntress shot venom and acid and gave Jasmine electric shocks and Jasmine tried her best to deflect it all.

"Let's go, Huntress. Are you even trying?" Jasmine asked, dodging a few punches.

*"**Pyrolineum**!" she called out, aiming a column of fire at her. The fire surrounded her and then she was just...gone. "What the—" Huntress appeared in front of her in a split second and roundhouse kicked her in the face, sending her flying through a glass building across the street.*

94. TITAN

Civilian evacuation was easy, look for people, find people, move people and repeat. It was easy for anyone really, but easier for someone with super speed.

After civilian evacuation, Arion went to take on the most powerful member of *The Superiors*, Rage.

Arion found him pretty easily. He just had to follow all of the damage and destruction that was happening around him. It was the gas truck that really surprised him though. He ran down the street at normal speed and saw Rage hefting a gas truck into his arms.

"Oh, no," Arion whispered. "No, no, no!" Rage aimed for the Air Canada Centre, directly beside the CN Tower, and then he threw.

Arion waited until the truck was directly above him and then he blew out a huge gust of air from his lungs. It sent the truck higher and higher into the air before he blasted it with his solar vision. The explosion shook buildings and shattered windows.

A fist flew at Arion's face and he didn't even remember blacking out.

He woke up about a kilometer away from the CN Tower and was being hefted into the air by a huge, gray hand wrapped around his neck. "This thing is going to happen whether you want it to or not, Titan."

Arion then got the unwanted feeling of being punched so hard that he flew through two buildings before slowing down enough to crash into a school bus.

Rage swooped in and pulled his wings inward a few meters above the ground. "There's only one way, Titan. Somebody is going to die today. And it ain't gonna be me!"

Arion threw a punch but Rage grabbed his arm and threw him into a car across the street. Arion just kept getting angrier and angrier until he heard a voice in his head say, *Focus, Arion*. It was a woman's voice but he couldn't tell if it was Jasmine. *You know he feeds on anger and fear. Just focus.*

Rage came at Arion again and he took every single punch. He pretended not to feel them, ignored them and just let his anger die down until he wasn't mad anymore, not even in the slightest. He wasn't sad or scared, he was happy. He knew that he could die fighting today but he also knew that it wouldn't be for nothing.

Rages punches grew weaker and weaker until Arion literally couldn't feel them. "What are you doing, punk?" Rage demanded.

"Kicking your butt," Arion yelled as he raised his foot and kicked him directly through the building in front of them.

95.   QUANTUM

Lucian weaved through all of the blasts that Nexus fired while absorbing Arcs electricity. In one quick swoop he knocked Nexus off of her feet but took a harsh shock from Arc. The shock was continuous as if he didn't intend to stop. That was up until a wave of sewage water washed over Arc and his gauntlets short circuited. He pulled them off quickly and threw them onto the ground.

Lucian was there, in a second and punched him straight in the head, knocking him out cold. "Thanks, Mer," he said as she rode in on a platform made of solidified water.

"Not bad, huh?" she asked. After a couple of crashes, they turned around to see a giant 80-foot tall Pixie coming towards them.

"Going up?" she asked. Lucian nodded and a chute of water shot out from under him and sent him barrelling through the air in somersaults until he steadied himself and controlled his flight. He was almost hit by an airborne Rage followed closely by a super-leaping Arion. Lucian shot dozens of energy blasts at Pixie and they seemed to bounce off of her, doing absolutely, *nothing*. Meredith was swaying around on her water-board and Pixie hit her, causing her to lose focus on her board and she fell.

Return to me! Lucian heard in his head.

"No, no, no!" Lucian yelled as the whole world morphed into a blur. He was standing back outside the front door of the orphanage that he was dropped off at when he was younger, before the group home. Everything shimmered as if it wasn't real.

He saw a man that looked strangely like his dad run up to the door and put a baby on the doorstep before banging on the door and running around the corner to where Lucian was. "This is something that you had to see," his father said.

"Why?" he demanded. "Why are you doing this to me!?"

"I brought you into the past to show you that *I* am the one that *allowed* you to be raised by the humans! I am your father and you will do what you are told!" Lucian quickly sparked with energy and his dad stumbled. "What are you doing?" he demanded.

"I'm not going with you! I have a life *here*!" he exploded in a small burst of red energy and his dad fell to his knees in front of him. "I have *greater* responsibilities now! I don't need to have training or be a god or even have *powers* to be a hero. And if you can't accept that...then you're missing the whole purpose of being a father!"

With one last blast of energy, Lucian broke out of whatever his father did to him and he reappeared exactly where he was before his dad took him away, him watching Meredith fall.

Lucian shot one more blast at Pixie and then swooped down, grabbing Meredith's arm and throwing her back up into the air. She easily used the water from the moisture in the air to create a new platform and secure herself.

"Thanks for the save," she whispered through his communicator.

"No problemo," he responded. "How do you want to take this?"

"You go high, I'll go low."

"Got it," he said. "You go first, I'll distract her." Lucian flew straight into Pixie's face and exploded in a small, bright burst of fiery-red energy.

96. CIRCE

Jasmine got up after being kicked through the building and flew directly at Huntress. Jasmine wrapped her arms around her and flew up as high and as fast as she could. "I don't have to breathe," she said. "You do!"

Jasmine broke through the atmosphere and continued on towards the moon. Jasmine threw Huntress into it and she rolled in slow motion. Huntress stood on the moon and clawed at her throat, unable to breathe. "I'm pretty sure whales can go an hour or two without breathing. It's either breathe, or fly out of here. You can choose." Jasmine flew back to Earth so fast that she nearly caught on fire.

She blacked out for a few seconds and when she woke back up, she slammed into Pixie's face going about a gazillion miles an hour which knocked the giant out cold.

"Where's Ar—Titan?" Jasmine asked. Lucian repaired her flaming clothes, just as Hyperion flashed in.

"3…" Lucian counted, "2…1," just as Arion smashed through a wall behind them. Rage took Arion by the foot and smashed him into the ground a few times before throwing him through 50% of the buildings in the city.

"Anybody else want some?" That was when Jasmine attacked. Rage slammed his giant fists into the ground which caused the whole ground to rumble and shake under everyone's feet causing them to fall. All except Jasmine, who was already in the air by the time he touched the ground. With a small blast of telekinetic energy, she made him stumble backwards and then caught him off-guard with a kick to the chest.

He fell back and did a somersault before landing on his feet. "That all you got, Princess?" he asked. In one swift motion, she kicked him in the stomach and he flipped over.

"Don't ever call me that."

"Sure thing, beautiful," Jasmine kept kicking him this time, getting angrier and angrier with each kick.

"Jasmine, NO!" she heard from behind her. Arion, she thought. One last kick but this time, he grabbed her ankle and flipped her around, slamming her into the nearest car. "It was all a distraction," Arion said, "The machine is going to go off unless we move it off of the planet."

"I got this," said Meredith, running. Just as she was about to leap onto a platform, a giant gray fist flew straight at her. Hyperion was the only one to react fast enough, appearing in-between Meredith and the fist.

Rage's fist flew faster than Jasmine's eyes could even process, punching a hole, straight though Hyperion's chest.

"SUMMONED!" Rage yelled. Arion leaped up and punched Rage so hard that he got knocked out cold.

Hyperion was on the floor, wheezing. The hole was sending out pulses of light every second, dripping golden blood. "The energy…" he wheezed. "It's going to blow. I'm going to die and I'm going to take Toronto with me, and surrounding cities, maybe all of Ontario."

Lucian's eyes glowed red for a brief second and he looked at Hyperion. "He's emitting too much radiation. He has the equivalent radiation of 5 nuclear bombs, maybe more. Meredith, get back, you can't withstand it." Lucian raised his arm and wrapped a red, glowing bandage around Hyperion's large wound.

"WAIT!" Hyperion called out before she left. "I'm sorry. For everything. For being a horrible teammate, horrible friend...horrible person. Meredith...I love you and I have since the moment I met you." Meredith had tears in her eyes.

"You'll be fine," she cried. "You're going to be fine!"

Hyperion reached up and brushed his glowing hand against her face. "Not this time, doll. Not this time. Get her out of here." Lucian raised his hand and a portal opened up under her, pulling her down through it.

"Hyperion, can you teleport out of here?" Jasmine demanded.

"No!" he yelled. He had another slight outburst of light, this time, shaking the ground enough to make them all stumble. "It's taking all of my power and my concentration to keep from exploding."

"Lucian," Arion begged, "Can you make a portal to outer space?"

Lucian shook his head. "Space is endlessly changing, too hard but I can get you pretty damn close. He only has a minute left, tops and the machine is going to go off—"

"I can do this," Arion whispered.

"Arion," Jasmine pleaded. "It's suicide!"

"Isn't that what we're supposed to do? Risk our lives for the good of the people? Isn't that why we *became* super-heroes!?" Arion countered. "I'm the only one fast enough to get away and if not, I can withstand it, and you guys know it! I got this. You guys get to that machine."

Lucian snapped his fingers and Titan's costume changed in a flash of red light. It looked almost the exact same except for the metallic tint. "I went over the formula of the materials that your suit was made out of and made it able to withstand nuclear explosions," he smiled weakly. "I guess we can test that out." Jasmine and Arion both stared at him. "It's what nerds do in their spare time! Your stares are disturbing my soul!" he jokingly yelled.

Arion nodded and shook his hand after giving Jasmine a

hug. He helped Hyperion stand up. "Can I get a boost?" he asked Lucian. Jasmine ran up to him and kissed him, flat on the lips.

"Come back, okay? Please?" He nodded and a giant multi-coloured portal appeared under his feet.

"I'm really glad I met you guys. Couldn't imagine my life any other way," he said before dropping through the portal.

97. <u>TITAN</u>

Arion soared through the air as he held on to Hyperion. He could tell that he wasn't really *flying*, he wasn't in control. He sped them up though, as fast as he could as they soared through the air. When Arion knew for sure that he couldn't do it, he asked a big favour of Hyperion.

"I need you to stop concentrating on not blowing up and give us some more lift. Just a bit." Hyperion closed his eyes and there was a small pop and they were teleported deeper in outer space. Arion floated next to Hyperion.

"You should get out of here," Hyperion said.

Arion put his hand on Hyperion's shoulder as they floated in space. "I'm not going anywhere," Arion sternly said. "We're in this together and I will make sure that you are never forgotten. Blake Gilbert, Hyperion. One of the new ages greatest and first superheroes."

Hyperion looked him in the eye and nodded. "You were scared to fly, right, man?" Hyperion asked.

"I was...now I just can't," Arion admitted.

"No, Arion. You can fly. This explosion is going to send you hurdling into space. I can't have you up here without knowing whether you can fly or not. Promise me that you'll get back to earth."

"I...I," Arion stammered, not sure if he could fulfil that promise.

"Promise me!" Hyperion yelled.

"I promise!"

There was one thing that Arion heard, after that, one thing that made everything worth it. In his head he heard one voice say, *Arion. I...I love you.* Arion could only smile as he realized that it was Jasmine, and then, Hyperion exploded.

98.   <u>QUANTUM</u>

Lucian put his arm around Jasmine as she cried into his shoulder. They watched Arion soar up into the sky. "Do you think he's going to be okay?" Jasmine asked.

Before Lucian could even answer there was a crack in the sky. It sounded like thunder multiplied by a thousand and it literally split the sky in half. All of the clouds were pushed aside and Lucian had to bite his lip hard to keep himself from flying off after them. "To be honest, Jaz...I really don't know," she started crying again. "You love him, don't you?"

"Don't be stupid, Lucian," she said with a forced giggle.

"Is that your way of saying: *If I tell you, I have to kill you?*" he asked.

"Something like that," she said.

"I think we should pass by his house...talk to his dad," Lucian suggested. Jasmine sniffled. "I can do it, if you want!"

"Are you scared of crying women, oh-so-fearless-Quantum?" Jasmine mocked. It sounded more like she was trying not to cry. Before Lucian could say anything, she said, "We should get to the machine."

They reached to the top of the CN tower and saw the machine on the top, with a glowing green force field surrounding it. "How do we do this?" Lucian demanded.

"Why do villains always put their bombs on timers?" she demanded staring at the clock. "Hey...I know that thing," Jasmine said pointing at a part attached to the machine.

Lucian examined it for a second. "That's a particle stabilizer, just a prototype from the looks of it but if *that* machine works the way that it's supposed to, then *this* machine is going to work perfectly. No one will die..."

"The Dot, an old super villain was auctioning it off. Sold to the girl in green—Huntress! Why is everything fitting together so...damned perfectly!?" Jasmine demanded.

"15 seconds." Lucian cut out the concrete surrounding

the machine and they tried to lift it but it wasn't even budging. "It's not working. Contain the blast!"

"3...2..." Jasmine and Lucian both put up force fields around the machine but it exploded anyways. A burst of energy waves erupted from the machine until it tinted the sky green, almost like a...green sunset. There were about a million jagged lines in the sky as different coloured lightning erupted in all different ways and patterns, spreading across the world.

"He was counting on us," Jasmine whispered. "And we couldn't do it."

99.   CIRCE

"We can't just leave him up there!" Jasmine yelled. "The machine already went off! We can't do anything about it! Let's go get him!"

"Jasmine, you saw that explosion," Lucian tried reasoning with her. "He's so deep in space that the only person that can bring him back is...well it's him. Only he can come back

when he's ready.

"All that we can do, is keep the team running. You're the leader of this team now, Jaz. What now?" he asked.

Jasmine sucked in a huge breath. "First, we talk to Arion's dad and Thalia and get Meredith...then we rebuild The Guardians. Better and stronger than before, so that if— when—Arion gets back, he can take the lead again."

Lucian nodded. He waved his hand and created a portal in front of them and Meredith hopped through. She punched Lucian in the arm. "Don't you ever try to save my life like that again, got it!?"

"Yes, ma'am!" Lucian said, throwing up a sloppy, mili- tary-style salute.

"Where's Hyperion!? Where's Arion!?" she demanded.

"They're...they're gone!" Jasmine cried.

ABOUT THE AUTHOR

Mylan Allen is a 15 year old student who lives just west of Toronto, Ontario. Ever since his first career choices struck out—Superhero, Genetic Lab Experiment, Super Soldier, etc.—he's been writing supernatural stories. *Gifted* is his first novel and will hopefully be a part of an enormous universe that he's putting together. He spends most of his time daydreaming and coming up with new ideas for dif-

ferent stories. He still has to go to school so he asks everyone to be patient with each novel. Follow him on Twitter at: *Guardian99Allen* for updates on The Guardians Saga!

Please, review the book online and help Mylan get out there. As a self-published author, it's difficult for him to market his books the way that other publishers and authors can. You can review it on: *Goodreads.com, Amazon.com, Amazon.ca, Amazon.co.uk and* even just by letting your friends and family know.

Glad you enjoyed the book, and Thank You!

Coming in **2016**:

UNCHARTED

The Second Book of **The Guardians Saga**